# LONDON



# Sharp and Short Volume II

## Five Stories Featuring DI Harry Hawkins

Garry and Roy Robson

# London Large: Sharp and Short Volume II



Published by London Large Publishing

ISBN 978-1-9993153-8-2

For more copies of this book, please email: info@londonlarge.com

# Contents

# Harry Walks into a Bar

# London: 1986

Harry Hawkins barrelled into the Frog and Nightgown on the Old Kent Road, more than ready for a good night out. He was relishing his first month as a murder detective, thrilled at the skills he was learning and the insights he was gaining into how murder inquiries were conducted. One thing was beyond certain, though, and that was murder inquiries were thirsty work. He was gagging for a pint of one of London's finest ales and ordered up a chaser scotch as an accompaniment as soon as he reached the bar.

His adoring wife, Julie, was out on a hen night, which meant he was a free man for the evening and that freedom meant that as the night wore on he would switch locations and visit one of his favourite haunts, sharing the banter with some long-time friends. For now, he just wanted to relax in and listen to a band who did a regular stint at the Nightgown, and who he'd seen a couple of times before. *Harry and the Hatstands* specialised in the crooner classics and old-school cockney favourites he loved. The band was tight and the lead singer, his namesake, could knock out a half decent tune.

He handed over the money for the drinks to the barman and took a seat at a table in the middle of the pub, nodding to one or two acquaintances before taking out his paper, turning to the sports pages and settling down to wait for the entertainment. The pub was busier these days than it used to be thanks, he assumed, to the growing local reputation of the *Hatstands* and the pub's recent facelift – although the new tables and chairs and the lick of paint hadn't exactly turned the place into the Café De Paris.

He studied the horse-racing pages with one eye and with the other observed one or two differences in the evening's clientele, coupled with a change in the usual relaxed atmosphere. He wasn't too concerned: the Old Kent Road, for so long a hidden London gem with over 32 drinking establishments along its two-mile stretch, seemed to have picked up a reputation in some far flung corners and visitors from Europe and beyond were turning up to sample its delights.

***

She was nineteen, maybe younger. Blond, blue-eyed. Definitely not English. The English girls were rounder, plumper and didn't have the intense eyes borne of a life of hardship. She'd seen things they hadn't. Probably Russian, if he was any judge, who'd used her looks and womanly wiles to escape from the place. She was sitting with a man much older than herself, but they were not close together. A sugar daddy indulging his young mistress? H didn't think so, on the basis of the body language, but it was possible. The man had a stern, dead-eyed look, and gave the impression he could handle himself if things turned nasty around him. H put him down as man who'd done time in the Soviet Army.

The girl put up her hand, clicked her fingers and ordered another bottle of wine. The Old Kent Road wasn't the kind of place in which table service was easily found, but the barman obeyed. She wasn't asking for change. She flirted with him when he delivered the drinks, smiled and ran her hands through her hair. To the casual observer she was having a good time, but an observant onlooker could see beneath the bluster. She was tense, hiding her insecurity behind bravado.

H looked around instinctively for more information and noted, standing near the exit and to the left of the stage in an unlit part of the room, two more men that needed looking at.

These were two big, formidable-looking lumps attempting to look inconspicuous, without much success. They didn't belong here. H joined up the dots in his imagination: these were likely bodyguards, minding a daughter with a heavyweight politburo father, or a mistress with a powerful benefactor. Maybe she was bored with Mayfair and the West End and just wanted to see some of the edgier parts of London.

***

The kid was sixteen, seventeen at a push. The pubs and clubs of the Old Kent Road were not the kind of places where they asked your age, not if you had enough money to pay for what it was you wanted. He looked to H like he had a wad of cash burning a hole in his pocket, and he was looking for action. His idea of action tonight was the blonde – he couldn't take his eyes off her.

She was returning his gaze, smiling, raising her glass with a wink, blowing kisses like they didn't have a price attached. The opportunity was too good for the boy to let it pass. H, taking all of this in with his fast-developing copper's eye, could see the kid was underage but was familiar with the landlord's policy with the youngsters in the pub: turn a blind eye and take their money until they lose control and start going at one another with broken beer glasses.

H looked on – he'd given up on the Racing Post now in favour of the drama unfolding, or about to unfold, before him – as the blonde bombshell blew the kid another kiss, twirled her tongue around her lips and sucked two of her fingers in a gesture that left little to the imagination.

The two men in the shadows looked on, their agitation evident, their body language showing the kind of signs that H always knew – had always known – were precursors to violence. Fidgeting hands turning to clenched fists, eyes scanning, assessing, the two men communicating with each other, labelling a target with eye movements and slight nods of the head. The likelihood of the kid getting beaten to a pulp here was high, H noted ruefully. The kid might have been a handful on Saturday afternoons chasing visiting football fans up and down the Old Kent Road, but he was not in this league.

***

The band took up their positions, looking like they'd been put together by a half-mad impresario with a sense of humour, after they'd been rejected individually at a low-rent talent competition in a pub worse than this one. The drummer was a sixty-year-old tub of lard with a wisp of grey hair and a little black leather waistcoat who looked like he still lived with his mother. The guitarist looked like he'd done more drugs than Keith Richards, and the bass player was a six-foot-four lunatic in some sort of shimmering Blaxploitation outfit – Earth, Wind and Fire would have rejected him for being too flash. H, though, didn't care too much about image and was pleased when Harry himself, looking as usual like a middle-aged bank manager done up as Rod Stewart for a fancy-dress party, took to the stage and brought everyone to attention. The band sparked up Adam Faith's sixties classic *What do you want?* H gulped the rest of his pint and hummed along.

*What do want if you don't want money?*
*What do you want if you don't want love?*

***

She downed a glass of wine, ordered up another bottle and indicated to the kid that he should come and join her. He didn't need asking twice and took his seat at the table between her and poker-faced guardian man without so much as glancing at him. She poured him a glass and ran her fingers through his hair. It was time to get merry and bright. The kid seemed too sozzled already, careless and driven by his hormones to take any notice at all of the man sitting next to him, or to notice the two men in the shadows.

Harry and the Hatstands ripped with great gusto into Andy Williams' *Happy Heart.*

H looked on and surmised that she'd have to pay a visit to the girls' room soon, at the rate she was knocking back the vino collapso. H stood up and made his way across the floor, weaving his way through the growing throng of dancers, and went through a door that opened onto a bare, cold corridor which had not been treated to the same uplift as the rest of the establishment. He walked along it to the two doors at the end. The left one said Gents. The right one said Ladies. H went right. He'd been into his fair share of women's toilets before – as a younger and in-demand man on nights like this, in places like this – and noted as he had on previous occasions that it was cleaner and less malodorous than its counterpart across the corridor. He checked that it was empty, plotted up in one of the cubicles, and waited.

***

She wasn't far behind him – about three or four minutes, H made it. He heard her enter the cubicle next to his, waited for her to finish her business, and was standing next to the sinks by the time she came out of the cubicle. She didn't seem surprised to see him there and was certainly not made anxious by his presence. She moved nonchalantly past him, turned on a tap and began washing her hands.

'Leave him alone.'

'Who fuck are you?'

'That doesn't matter. The boy, leave him alone. You know no good will come of it. Your goons should pick on someone their own size.'

'Fuck off. You know nothing.'

'Who are you?'

'I said fuck off. Get out of way.'

H moved aside as she walked to the door, went into the corridor and walked back towards the bar. As irritated as he was, H had never used force against a woman, and he wasn't going to start now.

***

The two of them were smooching to *That's Amore* by the time H returned. He made his way to the bar and stayed there while he drank another pint – his last for a while, as he'd need to be focussed. He watched all the players in the imminent drama and tried to consider his options, but the drink put him in a slightly more reflective mood. Was it any of his business? Should he let it go? No law had been broken.

Then things changed, quickly. The blonde put her coat on, grabbed her dance partner by the hand and pulled him quickly towards the exit, laughing aloud like a young girl who'd just downed a bottle or two of wine and was about to let rip.

Guardian man got to his feet and followed her out. The two thugs emerged from the shadows and followed him. H downed his pint and followed them.

***

The London night was clear and cold when H breasted the pub door. He ignored the biting wind as he swivelled his head left then right to see the direction of travel of those just in front of him.

That's when he knew he'd got it wrong.

It was a kidnap operation. Why hadn't he realised?

Almost in unison both shadow men drew guns from holsters inside their jackets and pointed them at the girl's protector. One told him to put his hands up. The other pistol whipped him, bringing his gun down hard upon his skull in three rapid strikes. The girl's minder fell to the ground. A black Mercedes pulled up as the pretty boy grabbed the girl by the hair, pulling her downwards, trying to force her towards the car. She screamed and kicked as she was dragged across the concrete, doing everything she could to resist.

If H was going to save her it had to be here and now; kidnapped young rich girls, he knew, seldom made it. He figured the kid was not much of a threat, so he could leave him to last. He wasn't armed, so surprise was his best weapon. The other two weren't expecting him – he put his head down and ran at them like an enraged bull, hard and fast.

The girl continued screaming and lashing out, valiantly increasing the energy and tempo of her resistance. She knew what H knew – it was escape or die. The big man surged past and bundled into the armed men. He punched one hard in the gut and the other harder, on the chin, before they could get their gun-hands organised. Neither went down. He grabbed one by the neck and pulled him along, knocking his gun from his hand in an attempt to snatch it. The gun clattered onto the concrete pavement. H tightened his grip, wrapping his arm around the man's throat and pivoting to ensure his victim's body now faced the car, the girl and the other man with the gun. His captive was resisting, thrashing madly as H tried to maintain full control.

The boy lost his nerve, released the girl and dived into the car.

H pulled his man to the ground, in the direction of the dropped gun, which he retrieved with a smooth rolling motion, never allowing the remaining gunman a clear shot – which forced him to take took another course of action: he grabbed the girl and pointed his gun at her head, just as H took aim with his newly acquired weapon, whilst still maintaining a vice-like grip around his victim's throat with his spare arm.

'Release him, or I shoot girl now.'

Standoff.

H stared at the man. He'd follow through. No doubt about that.

'We can all get out of this alive. Stay calm.'

'Release him. Now.'

'OK, listen to me. We've got two options here. Option one: You shoot her, I shoot you. Two dead. Option two: You release the girl, drop the gun, back nice and gently into the car. I let your mate here go, you both fuck off and crawl back under the rock you came out from. Everyone lives. Your call.'

H stared again at his adversary, who quickly decided to take option two-point-five. He pushed the girl forward and backed towards the car. He didn't drop his gun but instead aimed it at H as he backed into the car.

H relaxed his grip on the neck of the man he'd been struggling with, who ran and clambered into the back of the car to join his fellow kidnappers.

'Drive,' he screamed before the door was shut. H watched the car speed away, turn into nothing more than little red dots as it vanished into the London night.

He turned to assess the condition of the girl. She was bent over the damaged body of her would-be protector, fear and anger flashing simultaneously in her eyes. The anger won.

'Who is he?' said H.

'My uncle. He's hurt. He needs ambulance.'

H was right about one thing, at least. The accent was definitely Russian.

'They'll be one along soon enough. Who are you?'

'Alexandra Probotkin.'

'Well, Alexandra Probotkin, what's going on?'

H listened as Alexandra told her story at breakneck speed. She was the daughter of a high-level diplomat stationed at the Soviet Embassy in Kensington Palace Gardens. She was in a posh finishing school somewhere on the south coast. The man on the ground was her uncle, in town on a short visit. Daddy was too busy to entertain him properly, so she volunteered to show him the sights. He wasn't a London Zoo-Buckingham Palace-Tower of London type guy. End of story.

'How did you end up in this place?'

'We drive around. I like to see real places. I liked name...of *Elephant and Castle.* And pubs, *World Turned Upside Down*, and *Frog and Nightgown.*'

'What were you doing all the way down here without anyone to look after you – someone professional? Why didn't you have proper security? You must know people like you are watched, targeted all the time.'

'We did. Uncle lost them. They in car behind, uncle drive away from them. He wanted holiday…holiday from security, bodyguards, spies. He say he can see that in Moscow.'

***

H heard sirens wailing in the distance. He didn't want to be around when his own people turned up – there'd be too much explaining to do, too much hassle. Forms to fill out, interviews, justifications to be made. He looked hard at the girl; she was fine… and she'd have a story to tell. And at the end of the day all her uncle had suffered was a few clumps on the head. A few stitches would sort him out.

H pocketed the gun, straightened himself out and made ready to leave the scene.

'Who are you?' said Alexandra Probotkin.

'Your friendly neighbourhood spiderman,' said H, hailing a cab, 'at your service. Just be more careful next time. Don't run away from the people trying to protect you.'

He jumped into the cab. 'Just run me down to the Elephant, will you, son?' he said to the driver, 'and let's not hang about.'

The journey took three minutes. H jumped out of the cab and slipped into the *Charlie Chaplin*, to join the hardcore boozers enjoying a lock-in. 'Oi oi!' one wag shouted as he approached the bar, 'here he is, Inspector Jack Regan… better late than never.'

H ordered up a round of drinks for everyone and joined the circle.

'What's happening, son?' said his Uncle Arthur. 'Nicked any murderers yet?'

'Nah, not yet, I've only been at it a month,' said H. 'But I'll fucking nick you in a minute if you don't behave yourself.' He drank his scotch, chased it down with a big long gulp of beer, and said, 'Anyway, Art, I interrupted you. Sounded like you were telling a joke when I came in.'

'I was, son…I was. I'll start again at the beginning for you: a man walks into a bar…'

# On Margate Beach

# Kent: 1994

*'Down to Margate, don't forget your buckets and spades and cozzies and all...'*

Harry Hawkins wasn't a great fan of 'cockney crooners' Chas and Dave, but he was enjoying the atmosphere and sense of camaraderie built up by the duo's classic ode to day trips to the Kent seaside. Most of the day trippers had already boarded the coach he'd hired and were belting out the song in tune to the sound system, although some of the passengers were slightly more in tune than others.

Bobby, son of H's closest friend Ronnie Ruddock, had demanded a last-minute trip to the boy's room and H watched in amusement as he sauntered, without a care in the world, out of the service station toilet. H's wife Julie was holding the young lad's hand, urging him to hurry-up, she being rather more aware than him of the twenty or so people on the coach who wanted to get on with their day out.

As Bobby approached the coach H bent down on one knee, which triggered the youngster to run full-pelt and launch himself at his 'uncle'. H swept him up in his arms, swivelled round and deposited him inside the coach in one smooth motion.

'Come on son, time to get to the seaside,' he said. Julie, now six months pregnant, brought up the rear. She'd taken on the mothering role for Ronnie's kids because Ronnie's own wife had declined the invitation to join them – she didn't like to be seen with her husband's old friends, who, she felt, were mostly beneath her. H sometimes wondered what she saw in Ronnie, apart from the fact he was making a ton-and-a-half of money in the City and now dressed and looked like a film star.

When Julie reached the coach, H held her hand as she stepped unsteadily onto the vehicle and made her way to her seat. H climbed the coach steps to follow her in and was met with a chorus of good-natured pantomime disapproval.

'Oi, oi! About time, driver!'

'Come on, Harry boy, can we get going here or what?'

H took it all in good part, being it came from a well of deep affection for him and took up his position in the driver's seat.

'Can I go on the rollercoaster, daddy?' said Bobby

' 'course you can, son,' said Ronnie.

'Will you come on with me?'

'Yep, absolutely. And your uncle H will be having it as well, right H?'

'Yeah, course I will,' said H, who liked being called uncle to Ronnie's boys, even though he wasn't, not strictly speaking. He wasn't a great lover of fairground rides but knew well enough that the rollercoaster was mandatory. H ruffled Bobby's hair, fired up the engine and put the coach into gear. 'Margate, here we come,' he shouted as he pulled out from his parking position and back onto the M20 motorway.

Another Chas and Dave classic hit the sound system and the passengers raised their voices in appreciation. H would have preferred a bit of Sammy Davis, but he knew resistance was futile and so joined the newly formed coach choir in their rendition of *Rabbit,* a song dedicated to those women who felt it their duty to keep their men in check with a constant stream of nagging.

Julie gave him a sardonic smile.

***

Judy Jones didn't like the song. Judy Jones didn't like anything much. She sat on the other side of the aisle, two rows behind H, looking morose and disconsolate and refusing to join in the festivities. Maureen, her mother and Julie's elder sister, had insisted she come along to 'get her out of herself.'

'Get out of yourself! Get out of myself! What does that even mean, mum?' she'd said. 'For God's sake… all you lot ever talk is rubbish.'

Over the following days the request to join the day out caused a few more tantrums, some slamming of doors, and a refining of the art of teenage eye-rolling through constant repetition. Judy eventually relented during a visit from H and Julie, after he'd made a couple of corny jokes and said he'd miss her if she wasn't there. Judy liked H, found him both funny and sincere. More than that, she trusted him, and there weren't many people she could say that about.

Having agreed she returned to her room to listen to her Motorhead and Black Sabbath albums, which was a little unusual for a 13-year-old girl at the dawn of the Spice Girls revolution, but then Judy was not your usual 13-year-old.

Raising her had not been easy. Maureen, who hadn't wanted to rely exclusively on the welfare state to take care of family finances, had struggled for years, working a few hours a day in a local shop before returning home in time to greet Judy when she got back from school. Things became even more difficult when Maureen lost her own mother. That's when, even with the help Julie always gave, things started to get really tough. Financially they got by, but the emotional strain they were all under was a different matter, and Maureen found that keeping the family's secret from Judy was becoming increasingly difficult as the girl grew in maturity and understanding.

When Maureen looked at her daughter, behind the teenage moodiness and the quick-to-anger temper, she saw the pain in her eyes, borne of the confusion and uncertainty she carried within herself. She saw love too, but it was a love that was caged and gnarled and could not break through the scar tissue to be given.

'OK, sweetheart, seatbelt on?' said Maureen.

She'd become so used to her daughter's scowl and rolling eyes that she'd given up even mentioning it anymore, so she just rested her head on the rear of her seat and closed her eyes.

***

'Are we there yet?' said Bobby for the umpteenth time.

'Nearly, son, nearly. Another fifteen minutes,' said Ronnie as he took out a packet of liquorice all-sorts from his pocket and handed his boy one of the round coconut ones.

'Hmm. These are my favourites, dad. Lucky you got these ones.'

'Yeah,' said Ronnie, with a huge smile, 'lucky, that.'

The passengers were mostly in high spirits and enjoying the ride. Bobby's sister, Gill, was fast asleep, snuggled up in comfort on her father's shoulder, and two-year-old Little Tommy – son of H's brother Jimmy and his wife Sue – was likewise nuzzled deep in his own father's protective arm.

'Can we have something other than this Chas and Dave mockney bollocks,' shouted John Viney, another of H's old friends, from the rear seat.

'Stop moaning, you miserable git,' said H.

'Are we there, uncle H?' said Bobby

'Two more minutes, Bobby.'

They were on the outskirts of Margate now and, as H swung left off Union Crescent and headed for the car park he knew from previous visits, there it was: the sea. As if by magic the sleeping children woke up and stared with the usual awe and wonderment the sea always triggers in city kids. They looked on in mounting excitement at the beach, which seems to stretch out in all directions as H turned the coach and pulled into a parking space. This was, in a way, a high-point of the day for the adults too – taking in the view of the beach and the rippling sea. They looked like old and constant friends, chatting together as the waves broke gently, as if to soothe and reassure the sand that everything's just as it should be, as it's always been.

'We're there,' screamed Bobby, 'we're there!'

***

Jake Armitage woke up, and stretched out his frozen, aching body as best he could. It was a warmish day, but he was chilled to the bone. He was always cold now. The next worst thing was the isolation, the relentless loneliness. He was in the doorway of a boarded-up shop in Duke Street, a stone's throw from Margate beach. The shop, like the town, had seen better days and had once done a roaring trade selling Margate-themed nick-nacks and beach stuff to the hordes of holiday makers who no longer came.

Jake looked about him and wondered how he was going to get through another day. Some begging would raise enough for a tea or coffee, which he could cup his hands around for some momentary but illusory warmth. Then there was some decent grub available at the soup kitchen on the edge of town for the evening meal. He'd get enough to fill his belly.

But what was he going to do, all day long? He'd had a friend for a while, Willie from Glasgow. They got on well, the two of them. They'd both served, both seen action. But poor old Willie had suffered a massive heart attack two weeks earlier following a vodka binge and died in hospital. Jake learned of Willie's fate from a man at the soup kitchen. He never went to the funeral, though he supposed there must have been one, of a sort.

Almost more than the cold, then, it was the loneliness that was breaking him down, withering his life-force, destroying his will to live. He stirred and felt a twinge of pain in his right leg, the aftermath of being stabbed with a pen while he'd slept on a park bench in London some months previously. The streets of Margate were a lot quieter, and he hadn't been assaulted in a while – unless you counted the boozed-up late-night revellers who urinated on him while he slept.

He took two pictures out of his pocket, the only things he had left that connected him to his past life. One of them was of him and a few army buddies toasting the fact they were still alive after returning from a tour of Northern Ireland in the early 1980s. He'd loved the army. Serving in it had given him the best years of his life, the closest bonds he'd ever felt. The other picture was black and white, and faded. On this occasion he chose not to look at it. Sometimes it was just too much to bear.

He returned the pictures to his inside pocket and thought again about the day. He was a big-framed man who, in a previous life, hadn't scared easily. But as well as the cold and the isolation he also had the fear to contend with. He was always frightened now; frightened of the abuse and the hunger and all the pointless, empty time – and frightened, too, by things he couldn't name.

He felt, in moments of clarity when he was being honest with himself, a weird but unconcerned sense that he was getting near the end. He'd felt that way for several weeks now…or was it months?

***

Julie laid out a beach blanket and H and Ronnie found some stones to secure it against the gentle breeze that blew in from the sea. Before long the whole south-east London contingent had spread out around them. It wasn't a majestic day; there were no boundless blue skies or glorious sunshine, but neither was it freezing cold. Nobody's teeth were chattering, and the clouds broke and afforded them all a glimpse of the sun from time to time.

'At least it's not raining,' said Maureen. That was the main thing, they all agreed – as long as the rain held off, they'd have a great day.

Julie opened a cool box, affording those around her a tantalising glimpse of an array of goodies, and said, 'H, why don't you and Ronnie take the kids for a swim? I'll get the food ready.'

H didn't need asking twice. There was a flurry of activity as he, Ronnie and the rest kicked off their shoes and dropped their trousers to reveal a comical assortment of spindly white legs in shorts. H led the charge to the sea; Ronnie got started later but raced him hard and beat him to it; the kids scampered and screamed in after them, limbs flailing and laughing wildly. H and Ronnie made sure all of them got a good ducking.

'There's no point going in the sea unless you go under and get your swede wet,' roared H to the kids, '…am I right, Uncle Ron?'

This was all followed by a host of undirected games and activities, from building sandcastles to beach football and a bit of frisbee throwing.

After an hour or so of these frivolities H felt a rumble in the pit of his stomach and turned to see how Julie and Maureen were getting on. It was time for the real star of the day: the picnic. As if controlled by an unseen force the group movement towards the food began. No words were exchanged, but before long the entire party was hunkered around the feast like a flock of hungry seagulls.

There were cheese and ham sandwiches, peanut butter rolls, crisps of various flavours and, once the initial flurry of excitement was over, enough packaging whirling around the blanket to cover the coach they came in. Through this H saw a smidgeon of salad, which he declined to go for, and after a few sandwiches made his way to an area that had been reserved for desserts – sand-encrusted and looking the worse for wear, but still desserts. There was a Victoria sponge, a great mound of doughnuts and some Bakewell tarts.

'You've surpassed yourself here, love,' he said to Julie as he went to work on a decadent chocolate éclair that oozed cream onto his face as he bit into it.

'Blinding, that,' he said, 'absolutely fucking blinding.'

'H! Language! There's kids about!'

'Sorry, love.'

'Can we go to the funfair now?' the kids began to shout.

'Sounds like a plan,' said Ronnie.

'Ok. Let's get this mess cleared up and we'll…'

'Don't worry H, me and Maureen will tidy up. You all go on ahead.'

'OK, love,' said H, who didn't need much encouragement to give cleaning chores a miss, and walked off in the direction of town, like the pied piper, followed by a swarm of rug rats and their parents.

Julie and Maureen stayed behind, along with Judy, who had sat apart from the crowd and not condescended to eat anything.

***

Mark Turnbull, drunk as a lord, gathered up his bits and pieces, stuffed them into his plastic carrier bag and jumped off the train. He hadn't been to Margate for years, but even in his befuddled state he remembered the way to the beach. He rolled out of the station and onto Station Approach, choking back tears and hoping against hope that they'd be there, that he would be able to do what he'd come to do.

The going was hard, and he had to concentrate fully on giving the impression that he was a man who knew how to walk in a straight line. This didn't leave him with much capacity to think about anything else, but he did realise, as he rolled towards the Canterbury Road roundabout, that he'd made a bit too much of a pig of himself with those cans of Stella on the way down.

Coffee…maybe that was the thing. He would need to create a good impression – the one thing he couldn't afford to do was blow up all over the beach like Oliver Reed in the BBC's green room, getting geared-up before his big moment in front of the camera.

He found his way to the Promenade, hit the Wimpy Bar and ordered a large strong coffee and a Knickerbocker Glory. He spotted an empty table at the back of the place and set himself up at it. He needed to collect his thoughts.

It had been over a year now since Maureen had thrown him out, and he was still choking on it. He just couldn't get it down. He sat back and replayed the final, savage scenes again in his mind's eye.

'I'm sorry, babe,' he saw himself saying, 'I'm so sorry. It'll never happen again, I swear to you.'

'I don't care,' said Maureen through gritted teeth. 'I've been here before. There's no way back from this – the door's that way. Use it.'

'What about Judy?' he'd said imploringly as he was given his marching orders. 'She needs me… she needs a dad.'

'You're not her real dad. You could never be a proper dad...you're too weak. Go away.'

'How can you be so cold, after all we've been through?'

But Maureen had trusted before, and to trust again when trust had been shattered was no longer in her. Mark left, swearing an oath that one day he'd win Maureen back. But the breakup soon turned poisonous. In his sadness and anger he'd turned up drunk at her flat on several occasions, which forced Maureen into getting a restraining order that prevented him going anywhere near the place.

That had all been three months ago, three months since he'd seen Maureen or Judy, plenty of time to think about his life, cry over his self-inflicted misfortune and drink himself into oblivion many times over.

The coffee arrived. He downed it in one, burning his mouth, and asked for another. While he waited, he went to work on the Knickerbocker Glory. It tasted like his boyhood sure enough, but the memory didn't move or excite him. It just made him feel more tired. He felt like Old Father Time and had to resist a momentary urge to get out into the street and stagger back to the station as fast as possible.

But this was it. His last throw of the dice. He drank his second coffee, paid up, took a good, long deep breath and burst out onto the promenade just in time to see the sun disappearing behind a bank of clouds. The light was good, though, and once he'd made the beach it took him only a few seconds to locate Julie and Maureen.

'Hello girls,' he said, staggering across the beach towards them, smiling hard but looking as if he were on the verge of a breakdown. Maureen had seen the look before, and almost gagged on her slice of Victoria Sponge – she was as glad to see him as she would have been to have been presented with a cup of cold sick.

'How you been, love?' he said.

Maureen stayed rooted to the spot, the breeze moving her hair away from the cheekbones that had become so much more prominent in the year since she'd thrown him out. Her features warped slightly before she spoke.

'You shouldn't be here. I'd like you to go away. You'll upset Judy.'

'Marry me.'

'What? Are you insane? You're not even supposed to be within three-hundred yards of me. Go away, or I'll go and find a policeman to take you away.'

'Marry me. I want you back, I need you back...let's just get married, and get back on track. I'm ready – I've sorted myself out.'

The words fell out of his mouth gently but landed in her gut like an explosion of shrapnel, destroying her composure, filling her with rage and hatred.

'Sorted yourself out? You could have fooled me,' she screamed. Now they were at the centre of attention, but Maureen was past caring. She threw what was left of the Victoria Sponge at him, and carried on: 'Just go away – take a look at yourself, Mark, you're no better than your useless, piss-artist of a father. You're a disgrace. I wouldn't marry you if you were the last fucking man on earth.'

Judy, sitting with her eyes closed on the edge of the picnic blanket deep inside the music her headphones were pumping into her, became aware of the new arrival, looked up, and was filled with disgust.

To Judy, Mark had been just the latest in a series of 'uncles' and 'boyfriends' that had littered and polluted her life, though she did have a particular dislike of this one from day one.

'I don't like him. He's creepy,' she'd said the first night he'd been round.

'Give him a chance, Judy, just give him a chance.'

The disagreement with her mother burst into a full-scale row. It wasn't that Judy just hated Mark: she hated all of them, she hated the very idea of them. Why did they even have to exist? Eventually, the argument got to its deepest source.

'Why have you never told me who my dad is, where he his? I don't care about your boyfriends, I don't want any of them here. I hate you, mum, I fucking hate you.'

Maureen was a strong woman. She'd done her best and felt she didn't deserve this. As the argument gained more momentum Judy's anger reached its peak, and she spoke words she could never take back, although she'd wished countless times since that she could.

'You're a slag, mum. A whore, a dirty fucking whore.'

Maureen broke down. Having her daughter think and speak like this was too much.

Judy remembered her mother crying, her face like the rag doll she'd seen on TV. Rosie, her name was. Rosie and Jim – they lived on a canal boat and had lovely adventures. Why couldn't her life have been like that? What was the point of being a grown-up, she thought, if you couldn't make things nice? They were meant to be in charge – what was the point of growing up if you couldn't control things? She'd rolled her eyes, as usual, and walked out.

And now the bastard was back, arguing again with her mother.

Judy just wanted to blot the whole thing out, so she did. She turned and stretched herself out on the blanket with her back to the action, turned up the volume on her Walkman and went back into the music. It was, she felt, the only friend she had. Apart from Uncle H.

***

'Dreamland, what a name,' thought H, as he entered a place that promised so much and delivered so little. Most of the rides that he remembered as a young boy when he visited in the sixties and seventies had gone, and the place had gone from being a wonderous place that almost lived up to its name to a faded dream from a bygone era.

In common with most British seaside resorts the public's decision to vote with its feet and go on package holidays to Spain and beyond from the seventies onwards had dealt it a near-fatal blow. The resort still got a fair amount of day trippers, but residential holidaymakers staying for several days, what H would have called the place's 'bread and butter', had disappeared, making it difficult for the town's authorities to maintain its infrastructure.

Or maybe, thought H, things were just different through adult eyes, when he saw the excitement that lit up Bobby's face, and the wide-eyed enthusiasm of the rest of his young charges. He found their enthusiasm uplifting.

'What ride we going on first, uncle H?' said the boy.

'You pick, Bobby.'

They started with the rollercoaster, then the big wheel. The four of them – H, Ronnie and his children – sat together in a pod at the most satisfying moment of the whole Dreamland experience, at the very top of the cycle, with a stunning view out over the sea, hanging up high and waiting.

'Your turn soon, H,' said Ronnie. 'Julie won't be long, by the look of her. Looking forward to it?'

'Yeah, 'course I fucking am mate. It's been a long time coming for me and Julie, so we're not bouncing around and counting our chickens, but I'm raring to go.'

'You're going to be a great dad, mate.'

H was still smiling when they got off the big wheel and allowed Bobby to drag them over to a contraption that had teacup-looking pods moving around a central pole but which, at the same time, spun on their own axis in the opposite direction.

'Don't much fancy this one, Ron. Can you do the honours, mate, while I have a little mooch about? I'll relieve you when I get back and take them on the scenic railway.'

'No problem, H. Come on Bobby, Gill. Your uncle H has got to go and see a man about a dog, it's you and me on this one.'

***

The homeless man sat on the pavement in the shadow of Dreamland. He wore an old green parka coat about two sizes too big, threadbare army-surplus trousers and a pair of old black boots with no laces in them. The baseball cap on the pavement in front of him had no more than a few coppers in it.

'Don't suppose you've got a spare grand in your skyrocket, have you, boss,?' he said as H passed him.

The request for a thousand pounds, straight out of his pocket, made H smile. It was a good line, his kind of line. Instead of passing the man by, or dropping him a pound, H suddenly found himself standing still, as a distant memory – the memory of a voice – made its way into the foreground of his awareness. He knew that Geordie voice. It was now more gravelly, deeper, but, unmistakeable.

He got closer to the man, crouched down, and looked. The hair was dishevelled, the face was thin and scabbed, and it hadn't been shaved for a while. But it was still him, still the face of the man who'd helped him through when the bullets whistled round their heads in South Armagh bandit country, not long after Bobby Sands and some of the other IRA hunger strikers had died in '81. It had been a good warm-up,

Jake always used to say, for the Falklands turnout the following year.

'Jake…Jake Armitage,' said H, not as a question because he had no doubts, as he witnessed the shock of recognition dawn on his old mucker's face. 'It's me, H…,Harry Hawkins. What the fucking fuck are you doing sat here like this?'

'H?'

H held out his hand to help the man to his feet. They hugged, both laughing at the sheer unlikeliness of it all, H ignoring the stench of stale alcohol-breath and staler urine wafting up into his face.

'How are you?' said H. 'How long's it been?'

'Well, a good ten years, I should think.'

'Yeah, all of that. Not being funny, mate, but time doesn't seem to have done you a lot of favours .'

'Long story, H.'

'Tell me it then,' said H, taking him by the arm, 'we can have one in the London Tavern, if it's still going.'

'It is,' said Jack, 'but they won't have the likes of me in there.'

'We'll see about that. A nice pint of Guinness'll do you the world of good.'

***

'You?' said Julie, looking warily at the state of the London Tavern and wondering for the thousandth time what drew her husband – a creature of habit, if ever there was one – to such places. 'What the…?'

It was her second big surprise of the day, and even more astonishing than Mark Turnbull appearing from out of nowhere, like a ghost of Christmas past and asking her sister for her hand in marriage. This was turning into a very strange day.

'Hello, Jules, how is it?' said Jake.

Julie didn't hug or even shake hands with H's long-lost buddy, trying not to reveal her disgust at the sight of this once likeable and formidable man.

'So how's life?'

'Good, it's good, Jake,' said Julie, struggling for words, 'and how the hell are you?'

'Well, I've been better, but OK . How's your sister?'

'She's alright,' lied Julie, now remembering why she'd come in search of H in the first place.

'H, listen – Mark's turned up.'

'Mark who?'

'Mark bloody Turnbull.'

'What? Turned up where?'

'On the beach, a little while ago. Looking for Maureen. He's acting up a bit…he's got a big carrier bag full of booze with him. He's just asked her to marry him.'

'Well fuck me,' said H. 'This is getting to be like an episode of *Alfred Hitchcock presents.* And here's me sitting with Jake Armitage. What are the odds? Jake, I'm going to have to deal with this, mate. Wait here, I'll be back soon. Get yourself another pint.' H pulled a wad of money from his pocket, peeled off a five-pound note, dropped it onto the table and left with his wife.

***

'Looks like there's going to be a few fireworks, mate,' H said to Ronnie when he and Julie got back to Dreamland.

'Why, what's happening?'

'Maureen's wanker of an ex-boyfriend has shown up, giving it large by all accounts.'

'What, Turnbull? What's he doing here?'

'We're just about to find out…and not only that. My head is spinning mate.'

'Why, what's happened?'

'I've only just gone and bumped into Jake.'

'What?' said Ronnie. 'Gateshead Jake?'

'Yep, the one and only.'

'Fuck me…talk about two for the price of one. Where is he now?'

'I left him in the London Tavern. Let me just sort this other little prick out and we'll go back to him.'

'I'll come with you now.'

'No, mate. You stay here. Keep your eye on the kids. I'm not in the mood to mess about with Turnbull – no need for the kids to see it all kicking off.

'OK mate…see you in a bit then.'

***

Julie struggled to keep up as H surged out of Dreamland and headed for the beach, and the cause of his agitation. When he spotted Turnbull wheeling around his party's beach blanket, singing – or rather shouting – at the top of his voice a song H couldn't make out, he broke into a trot, and then an outright run.

He arrived at speed, kicking up sand and by now shouting himself, and grabbed Turnbull by the shoulder. 'What the fuck are you doing here? You're meant to keep away, you know that.'

Mark Turnbull, spun around quickly by the force of H's shove, found himself face-to-face with Harry Hawkins, a man who'd always made him feel uneasy, even at the best of times. And this was not one of those.

'Just got the train down, for a day out. No harm in that, is there? It's a free country, ain't it?'

'Yeah, it is son. The hospitals are free as well, and that's where I'll put you if you don't fuck off right now. I don't care how you got here or what you want to do. Just get moving.'

Turnbull, still fired up and emboldened by the Stella, stood his ground.

'Who do you think you are? I don't give a flying fuck whether you're a copper or not. I can go where I please.'

In the background, H noticed out of the corner of his eye, Judy had taken her headphones off. To her the day was suddenly looking up. Mark Turnbull, at the end of the day, was just a bully, and she knew that all bullies back down when they're confronted by someone bigger than them. And Harry Hawkins was bigger than just about everyone she knew.

'Last chance, Mark,' he said. 'There won't be another one. Fuck off. Now. Get off the beach.'

'Listen,' said Turnbull, 'I said it's a free…'

H feigned a little punch. Turnbull stepped back, tripped over his own feet and fell to the sand. He got up, feeling humiliated, pulled a defiant face and started to move backwards across the sand.

Judy, smiling for the first time since they'd set off from Bermondsey, laughed as Mark Turnbull walked away, shouting profanities and threats of revenge against H to save what little face he had left.

'Right,' shouted H to the company at large, 'job done. I'm going back to talk to Jake.'

'Jake?' said Maureen. 'Jake who?'

'Well, how many Jakes are there?' said H.

'Probably loads,' said Judy, laughing loudly, 'in some parts of the world.'

But her mother was not laughing.

'Jake?' said Maureen. 'Jake Armitage? He's here? What…?'

'Yeah. Long story, darling – and I don't know half of it yet. But he looks to be in a bad way – he's been sleeping rough somewhere behind Dreamland.'

'Don't bring him here. For God's sake don't bring him here,' said Maureen.

'Why not? He's a good man – the best. He's a long way in front of that other lemon we've just got rid of,' said H.

'That you got rid of, H,' said Judy, with a smile.

'Yes, well…the thing is…you lot have no idea what people like him have been through. If you'd seen him in the Falklands…'

But this was no time for speeches. H turned on his heel and rushed back to the London Tavern, but by the time he got there his old friend was nowhere to be seen. The only trace that he'd ever been in the pub was a half-finished pint of Guinness on the table and the rotten smell of a man long unwashed. H flashed his warrant card about the place like he was on a proper investigation, asked around, and jogged up and down the street harassing pedestrians, but his Jake Armitage had melted away.

H returned to the beach feeling angry with himself for letting a chance to help an old friend slip through his fingers. Mark Turnbull was long gone, but everyone else was present. Another sprawling game of football was in progress. H got involved, so that everyone was playing, apart from Maureen who remained sitting by the group camp, feeling pensive, and Judy and Julie, who were having a heart-to-heart as they walked along the shoreline.

Julie noticed with pleasure the improvement in her niece's mood after H had seen off the least favourite of her 'uncles'.

'So,' said Judy, being remarkably human and expansive, 'do you know the sex of the baby?'

'No. We decided we'd prefer a surprise.'

'I think that's better. Keeps the excitement going. Have you got names ready, for a boy or girl?'

'Well, if it's a boy then H will insist on calling him Ronnie.'

'After his mate? I can see they're really close.'

'They are. They were in a battle together, in the Falklands. Ronnie saved H's life. And long before that they were best mates as boys, so...'

They walked and talked some more about things they'd never talked about before.

'Any boyfriends on the horizon?' said Julie.

'No,' laughed Judith, her cheeks flushing, 'I'm not interested.'

'You will be.'

'Well, if I was, I'd want a boyfriend like your husband. You're very lucky.'

Julie laughed.

'…and your little Ronnie, or whatever, he's going to have such a great dad.'

'Yeah,' said Julie, 'I know.'

A sudden eruption of screaming and shouting reached them from a distance.

'I wonder what all the commotion is?' said Julie.

'Over there,' said Judy with a wave of her arm, 'it seems to be coming from over there.'

It was a long way off, but Julie could make out someone pulling a body out of the water. H and the others were closer, and she could see him and Ronnie sprinting to the source of the commotion. They started to walk towards it. A large circle had formed by the time Julie and Judy got there, and inside it, at the centre, she saw her husband pushing down rhythmically on the chest of a prone man. Julie moved closer, until she could hear Ronnie talking quietly into H's ear.

'He's gone, H…he's gone.'

H fell to the sand, exhausted and in despair. To find a lost friend and see him taken in the space of two hours was too much. Death followed him everywhere, it seemed, even on his days off. He and Ronnie hugged above the body of their fallen comrade. Julie shed a tear. Maureen, arriving late to the scene, broke down in an uncontrollable fit of crying.

***

The murky grey sky was now bringing in a faint drizzle from the sea. Judy moved away from the madness of the crowd. She sat down, alone on the blanket, and thought about the day. A motley crew of Londoners on a day trip, looking for fun and relaxation. Mum's ex turning up from nowhere, asking for her hand in marriage, only backing down when H threatened to knock him out. Then a drowned man she'd never seen before tops himself and it ends uniting the adults in grief.

What a mess. Just like her life. With all her heart she ached for a real family, a restored family, a family with nobody missing and nobody completely fucked up. She longed for a strong, healthy family as only a child who never had one can. She began to cry, gently, and watched unknowingly as H and Ronnie helped the paramedics pick up the body of her father and carry him to the ambulance parked up at the back of the beach.

THE END

# Peter Brady

# Dagenham: April 2001

The series of events that turned Peter Brady into a different kind of man began just over a year before his final transformation. A little after returning home from work one evening he received an unexpected call on the mobile phone his wife had bought him the previous month. The voice on the line informed him he was talking to his company's HR manager. He'd worked at the sharp end of car production for over 20 years and, as far as he could remember, had never met nor so much as known the name of anyone in the HR department. As long as they paid his wages on time, and in that regard, they had an impeccable record, he had no reason to look them up. He was good at his job, he liked it, and that was enough.

'What do you think it's about?' asked his wife, Gill, after he'd finished the call.

'Don't know, love, maybe they're going to present me with a nice long-service bonus or something,' he said with an ironic laugh.

The next morning, instead of going straight to the production line of the Ford plant looming large on the horizon, to do his usual eight hours, he made his way to the company's office area adjacent to the main buildings. He found the room and was greeted with gushing over-enthusiasm by the HR man, who gave him a coffee, sat him down in a plastic chair and told him the news. Though he half-expected the worst, it hit him like a hammer and, as his stomach fell through the floor and kept on going, he tuned out. HR man's voice buzzed like a giant mosquito for a few seconds, and by the time Brady was listening again he was already doing the justifications:

'It's the Far East, Peter. You know what's happening over there. We just can't compete on price anymore. They can make our product for a fraction of what we can, even if you include transportation. Specifications can all be done over the internet now, so no need for any travel. We're sorry, but we have to do everything we can to survive. The company's moving a major chunk of production to China and downsizing here.'

This kid in the bad suit, who was no more than a messenger boy for the guys who'd made the decision, droned on about the generous redundancy package and the out-of-work support services, but again Brady wasn't listening. His mind was racing ahead, doing the life-maths, trying to figure out the odds of a redundant fifty-seven-year-old, semi-skilled, twenty five-year Ford man getting any kind of half-decent job. At best he'd be lucky to be retrained, given elocution lessons and stuck in a call centre for ten hours a day.

'We'll be alright, love,' said Gill when he got home and broke the news. 'I'll get a job down the supermarket or something, to top up what I earn at the salon,' she said. 'You know, until you get back on your feet.'

'Yeah, well, good luck with that,' Brady said sourly. 'Have you seen the statistics on unemployment for people our age? And even if you did get a job stacking shelves or whatever, if you add what you get out of that to your other job it still won't be anywhere near what we need for the mortgage, will it, let alone all the food and bills and that?'

Gill didn't know the ins and outs of the couple's finances, which she'd always entrusted to her husband, who did. He knew exactly how much he'd increased the mortgage by in order to pay for their new kitchen and the cherry red Audi TT 20 in the driveway, a car many believed, rightly, to be several notches above his pay grade. He'd loved it from the moment the model first appeared in 1998, and it hadn't taken him long to talk Gill around. He told her they could afford it, which was the truth, just about.

'Well, never mind love, I'm sure something'll come up,' Gill said, 'it always does.'

Brady kept his own counsel and tried to work out what would "come up" first: the sale of the house and the move to a little flat, or the sale of the car and its replacement with a nondescript mid-market saloon.

Both would come, he supposed, but the car would be especially hard to let go of. And they had no children to leave the house to anyway.

***

He didn't agonise over the decision for long, because his initial thoughts on the house v. car scenario paled into insignificance two weeks later, when the second in the series of events that changed his life occurred.

And then, six months later, came the third, as he sat in an Old Bailey courtroom awaiting a verdict.

'Not guilty, your honour,' he heard the jury chairman announce.

The words hit him like a bolt of lightning. How could this be? He sat with his head bowed as the judge spoke words that should never have been spoken.

'Constantin Spiru, you have been found not guilty of the charges brought against you. You are free to leave the court.'

Brady sat motionless as he tried to control the tempest raging inside him, and kept his head bowed as a smiling Spiru glanced in his direction and winked before walking out into the corridor, where he was met and congratulated by a gaggle of cheering friends, who high-fived and hugged him with great drama and passion before bursting out of the building and setting off on foot, laughing and shouting as they hit the street and turned into Limeburner Lane.

Back in the Bailey Peter Brady sat, slumped and motionless, unable to raise his head, unable to stand, unable to move. He was numb to the supporting arm of his lawyer when it was wrapped around his shoulders, emotionless in response to the words of his friends, dead to the appeals of the journalists pestering him for a comment.

It had come down to his word versus that of Spiru's former wife, Viorica. He knew he was right. He'd never forget the face of the man who plunged a knife deep into his wife's heart as he handed over the keys to the Audi TT. Spiru and his crew had dragged them from the vehicle at a set of traffic lights in Barking and Spiru's face was revealed when Gill, in her panic and her anger, tore his balaclava off, an act for which she paid the ultimate price. It was a face that had come back to haunt him every night since in his dreams, in which he would beg Gill to keep still and not make a move for the mask; but the dreamworld refused to bend and consistently replayed the truth, as he saw the woman he'd loved since he was twenty years old butchered.

He hadn't been on his game at any point in the process. The defence counsel had found out about his redundancy and used it against him, telling a tale of instability and depression that threw him completely off guard and made him look like a very sketchy witness, unlike Viorica Spiru, who was well-drilled, beautifully well-turned out and well-versed in the art of lying to and manipulating the hearts of jurors. His lawyer didn't seem to be able to touch her.

After a time, Brady remembered where he was, looked up, surveyed the scene and noticed the figure of Detective Inspector Harry Hawkins, who'd led the investigation, looking not much less morose than himself. They'd spent a fair bit of time together, the two of them, talking and looking through mug shots and all the rest of it, and had almost become close. This gruff-looking policeman had been sympathetic and left no stone unturned until he'd tracked down Spiru and done all he could to make sure the Crown Prosecution Service prosecuted the case vigorously.

'Peter, I'm sorry,' said H, looming up over him and extending a hand.

'How did that happen? I…what happens next?' said Peter.

'Nothing, Peter. That's it. We've done what we can. Spiru's old woman should get a job with the Royal Shakespeare Company, it was her word against yours in the end and it's hard to compete with a woman like that. And her brief, Oswald Carruthers, is the best there is at getting the members of a jury to feel like they're starring in a courtroom drama with Sir Laurence Olivier and turning their heads round. And, well, there's no DNA evidence, no other witnesses to back you up, no murder weapon. I've pushed every line of enquiry to its limits. I've done everything I possibly could to nail this, but without new evidence, there's nowhere left to go.'

'So that's it? I just accept that he kills Gill then walks straight out of court, while I go back home and…?'

H sighed heavily and shook his head in the affirmative. There was nothing he could do now for the shattered, hollowed-out man in front of him, so he pursed his lips and looked him in the eye but made no reply.

***

Brady sat in his house, with nothing to do and nowhere to go, alone except for his memories and pictures of his wife. In the three long months since the day of the trial he'd only been out on a few occasions, to the memorial park where he'd paid for a bench with Gill's name on it. Most of his friends had fallen away, which suited him just fine – he didn't want any company. Sharon from next door came by once or twice a week, bringing food and a little company. For a month she'd skirted around the edges of his pain, asking him if he was OK and checking the cupboard and fridge to ascertain the supplies he needed, which were not many. He was eating enough to keep himself alive, just, but was losing a lot of weight.

After the second month she felt comfortable enough with his grief to broach the subject.

'Peter, you have to snap out of it. There are people out there who'll help you. Why don't you see one of the bereavement support councillors' that came around? Let one of them in. It'll help you.'

'There's nothing they can do for me, Sharon. There's nothing any of them can do.'

'Well, at least try and eat a bit more. You're turning into a skeleton. Is that what Gill would've wanted – for you to just sit here and starve yourself to death?'

'We'll never know the answer to that, will we?' he said, forcing a mouthful of Sharon's home-made carrot and coriander soup into his digestive system, 'but thanks for the soup.'

'And what about all these letters piling up? You'll have to deal with them. There might be something important.'

'Nothing's important.'

Sharon ignored him and went through the letters as part of the larger project of doing her best to sort out his finances.

'Your redundancy money'll cover the mortgage for a few more months, but you'll have to get a job, or sell up in the end. The social security won't pay for a mortgage the size of yours.'

'I haven't asked for anything from the social.'

'Well you should. And what about the car? Have you thought of downsizing to something a bit more modest?'

'I'll cross that bridge when I come to it,' said Brady, rising to his feet and indicating with a sweep of his arm that it was time for his neighbour to head for the door.

'Thanks for coming round, Sharon,' he said, 'and for the soup.'

***

Uncontrollable daydreams of murder drifted in and out of his mind all day long. He'd wait outside Spiru's place until he emerged and load bullet after bullet into his face until it looked like something hanging in a butcher's shop window. He saw the corpse lying dead on the ground while he continued firing, splattering fragments of bone, grey matter and flesh and blood across the pavement. He fantasised about walking up behind Spiru with a machete and taking off his head with one clean, expertly delivered swipe of the blade; but that was too easy, there was no suffering there. The fantasy had to be reimagined. He'd sever the arms first, then make his man kneel and beg for his life before hacking repeatedly at his neck.

These and other scenarios of savage retribution occupied his thoughts in the moments he wasn't thinking of his poor wife's final moments. Every time he considered violent reprisal it energised him, and for brief moments he felt he could do it. He felt that he would do it. It wouldn't be hard to track down Spiru. He knew Hawkins had arrested him in Harlesden. He could hire a private detective. He didn't know any proper criminals personally, but he'd get hold of a gun from somewhere. How hard could it be?

But the chasm between thinking and doing was huge, and he never took an actual step towards action. Whether it was lack of courage or an inner moral compass that wouldn't let him take a life, he wasn't sure, but each time he reflected on his situation after a bout of bloody fantasizing he felt empty and dismayed. His shoulders would slump, his energy dissipate, and he'd be back in the swamp of despair from which there seemed no escape. He started to rot away, bitterness and hatred and self-loathing eating him up, like parasites consuming his body from the inside.

His wife would never get justice.

***

Sharon's visits became less frequent. He didn't blame her, he was becoming increasingly terse and off-hand, and anyway she had her own life to get on with. His survival instincts kicked in when she stopped coming around with food and he started visiting the shops a few times a week, stuffing a trolley with the cardboardy microwave meals that provided his sustenance.

Loneliness became his only friend, accompanying him morning, noon and night. He started to doubt what was going on in his surroundings. A creaking sound upstairs would fill him with dread. What was up there? His sleep patterns became erratic. Long patches of time went by in which he was nowhere but inside himself. At times he would become aware of the presence of his wife but refused to talk back when she spoke to him. She's not really there, she's dead, she's gone, he'd say to himself, refusing, just, to fall into a pit of insanity from which he sensed he would never emerge. He was on the edge of things.

***

One day, as he searched without much success for a clean cup amongst the detritus in and around his kitchen sink, his home phone rang. He didn't usually answer it, but the caller was persistent. The phone diverted the call to voicemail four times, but the caller rang back a fifth. This time he answered.

'Hello Peter, Harry Hawkins here. Can we talk?'

'Why have you called?'

'There's been a development.'

'What kind of development?'

'Viorica Spiru called me yesterday, out of the blue. Says she wants to change her story.'

A slither of hope tried to force its way into Brady's heart, but he fought it off.

'Why?'

'She's fallen out with her old man, or so she says. She's asking me for money, which we won't be able to give her, but I've arranged to see her tomorrow, to see what she has to say. Thought you might like to know. I'll keep you posted.'

Peter didn't whoop for joy or break out into a song and dance. He hung up the phone, found and washed a cup and made himself a coffee before returning to the sofa. He didn't feel any hope, there was no place left in his heart for it.

The next day, he was startled by an early morning knock on the door. It was loud and abrupt, not Sharon's little tap, or the bereavement councillors' chirpy rat-a-tat-tat. They'd given up on him long ago. Curiosity got the better of him and he opened the door.

Harry Hawkins blinked and took a second look when he saw the pitiful sight in front of him. Brady was around 40lbs lighter than he remembered, and as he stared into the eyes of the hollow man, he saw he'd crossed over to the other side and no longer gave a damn about anything that happened in this world.

'Peter,' said H, when he'd recovered from his moment of shock.

'Harry. You want to come in? The place is a bit…'

Brady opened the door wider and H walked in. The house was more than a mess, it was a disaster zone. Brady led the way to the kitchen. The place stank of an unholy combination of musty, unwashed male, cigarette smoke, stale coffee, unwashed dishes, stacks of discarded ready-meal packages and whatever it was that Gill Brady's now-deceased cat had left behind it. H left the kitchen and went into the sitting room, making his way across the tide of objects that littered the floor, which he remembered as a much more orderly place during his many visits to Brady over the course of his investigation. H had seen people go to pieces before – it was commonplace in his line of work – but this was off the charts. Brady was in deep and, though his heart was filled with pity for what the poor man had been through, H could only call things as he saw them. He knew no other way.

'For fuck's sake, Peter. This place is disgusting. You've turned it into a complete shithole. What's been going on?'

Brady ignored the question.

'Got news for me, then, have you?' he said.

'Yep. But it's not good. Viorica Spiru. I went to her place to have a word with her.'

'And?'

'She was dead.'

Brady slumped into an armchair. He said nothing for a time, while H watched him closely. It looked as if something was coming unmoored inside him, taking him to an even darker place than he'd become used to. H's instincts and long experience of dealing with people in pain told him this. Brady's face itself was as blank as the day is long. But beneath the surface…

'How?' Brady said at last, looking at the floor.

'Heroin overdose.'

'So, the last person in the world who can bring justice for Gill is dead?'

'Yes,' said H.

'Spiru did it.'

'You don't know that. But I'll investigate it.'

'You know, Harry, I've spent night after night and day after day fantasizing about how I could kill him. But people like me, we don't do things like that. That's why we need people like you. Now what?'

'Like I said, I'll see if I can find anything suspicious around this heroin overdose. There might be something, there might be nothing. But listen, Peter, you can't go on living like this. I'll send someone round, to help tidy up, get you back on your feet.'

H didn't always give the best advice, but it was the best he could do. He'd experienced post-traumatic stress disorder himself – and still had Falklands flashbacks, from time to time – so had some understanding of Brady's state of mind. Or thought he did.

'You have to let someone in,' he said over his shoulder as a parting shot. 'The house, I mean. I'll send someone round, but you've got to let them in.'

Brady closed the door behind him.

***

A little after the anniversary of his wife's death Brady woke up and checked the morning post. He'd started opening and reading letters, although he never took any action regarding their content, preferring to tear them up as soon as he'd finished with them. This morning the one he knew was coming had finally arrived, although the news that repossession proceedings to take control of his house had begun didn't concern him.

He had a savings account with a different bank from the one that held the deeds to his house, and knew that if he wanted to, he could ward off the day of reckoning for a few more months. But he didn't want to use the money for that.

'Fuck 'em, fuck 'em all,' he said to himself out loud.

The next day he got up early, showered and ironed a white shirt he'd washed the previous evening. He matched it with his best suit and polished the black shoes he hadn't worn for half a year. The suit fell off him in folds, making him look a bit like he'd just escaped from a circus, but it concerned him not one iota. He made his way to the shopping centre on Dagenham Heathway, went into the bank that held his private savings and asked to withdraw them in cash. It wasn't a fortune, just over eight thousand pounds. The bank teller said they didn't have that much, holding cash being something they were trying to reduce.

'I want cash.'

'Well, we can do it, but it might take a while.'

'How long?'

'A few days.'

'OK. I'll just take a grand for now and come back for the rest.'

He returned home and knocked on Sharon's door in the adjoining semi-detached. She was both pleased and surprised to see him looking more with-it and animated. He knew she had a computer with internet access, so he asked her to find some low-grade hotels and the phone numbers of local private investigators. Brady got what he needed, then sat back and got into his tea and biscuits.

'Sharon, you do have house insurance?' he said.

'Of course I do. What sort of question is that? Why do you ask?'

'That's great,' he said, and gave her a thousand pounds.

'What's this for? I don't want your money.'

'You've looked after me, you were the only one. Just take it. Please,' Brady said, then got up and left the house.

He returned to the bank a few days later with a shoulder bag, loaded it up with cash and then drove the cherry red Audi TT to his local garage. He filled the tank and brought a petrol can, which he also filled up. He drove back home and knocked on Sharon's door. There was nobody in, which was perfect because he didn't want to put her in danger. He might no longer have regard for his own life, but Sharon had been a decent neighbour.

'Good,' he said to himself. He went back to his car to collect the petrol can, returned to his house and poured the contents across his sitting room sofa. He pulled a box of matches out of the billowing pocket of his suit trousers, lit one, and threw it onto the sofa.

The blaze was already burning brightly when he got to his car. He put a few bundles of notes into his inside suit pocket, threw the bag of cash into the boot and drove off.

***

Leading Firefighter Phil Harding was first on the scene. By the time he arrived, the fire was well established and thick, black smoke-filled Brady's house. The temperature in the source room was over 600 degrees F. The fire had spread to the upper rooms and thence to the attic via a combustible soffit above a landing window. In the attic, it was energised by oxygen from a hole in the outside wall Brady had neglected to repair and fuelled by a lifetime's photos and assorted memorabilia. The space between his and Sharon's house was compartmentalised by concrete blocks, which might have been enough to contain the inferno if the seal between the top of the wall and the roof covering hadn't been made of mineral wool. The heat from this ignited a shared, combustible lining between the tiles and the roof structure. The memorabilia in Sharon's attic was also now fuelling the blaze.

Phil Harding could see the source-house was beyond saving and so would be anyone in it. He ordered three team members to knock through the door of the second house and search it. They returned empty handed.

Harding's unit hosed the area, concentrating on ensuring the blaze didn't spread to gardens or nearby houses, and the fire went no further. By the time the flames had died Brady's house was no more than a shell, and Sharon's was structurally unsustainable.

Two fire investigators turned up and confirmed what Phil Harding and his crew already knew. This was arson. The evidence was clear: tremendous scorching on one side of the living room, a tell-tale sign that a foam filed sofa by the wall had been doused in petrol or some other accelerant and set alight.

The protocol was clear. This was a serious criminal offence, and the culprit had to be identified and found. This was now the police's baby. Their inquiries would start, as always, with the homeowner.

***

Brady drove along the Westway towards White City in the Audi, keeping things nice and easy. He turned into the car park of a fast food restaurant, jumped out and made his way to the service area. He ordered a double-size bacon burger with all the trimmings, large fries, a large fizzy drink and added in a couple of pastries for good measure. He sat down and enjoyed the most calorific meal he'd had in a year and belched loudly with satisfaction after he downed the last of his fizzy drink.

He sat back, took out his phone and called Harry Hawkins.

'Hello, Hawkins here,' he heard a once-comforting voice say.

'It's Peter Brady.'

'Hello Peter. How's it going? What can I do for you?'

'I burnt my house down.'

'OK…uh, why?'

'Because.'

'Why are you telling me?'

'I broke the law, and you're a policeman. I wanted to tell someone the truth.'

'Fair enough. I'll have to call this in.'

'I know.'

'Where are you?'

'Ask me no questions and I'll tell you no lies. I just wanted to let you know.'

Brady ended the call, returned to his car and started on the next leg of his journey. By the time he was back on the Westway there was an all-points bulletin out on him, and police officers all over the London area had been advised of the description and number plate of the cherry red Audi TT being driven by a Mr Peter Brady, someone who was mentally unstable and possibly dangerous to the public.

***

PC Jack Pender was a good cop and had always been a top-notch driver. He'd managed to fit both his love for driving fast and his liking for the rough-and-tumble pursuit of bad guys into a career. He was bright but not ambitious and had done everything he could to dodge promotion and stay on the road, signing on as a 'Life PC' when it was still an option. He'd found his niche.

Motorway duty could be boring, on occasion, but once in a while he had a great day doing the things he adored on or around the M1. The last few days had been uneventful, a couple of minor crashes on his patch and a few boy racers having chariot races in the fast lane had been about it. The lack of action drained his energy at times, but he knew it wouldn't last – people being people it wouldn't be long before some miscreant would give him and his partner, Gideon Olavarria, something to get their teeth into.

It was mid-morning on the post-rush hour motorway when his onboard software matched the number plate on a passing red Audi TT to one of interest to the forces of law and order. He perked up, downed his coffee, handed Olavarria his cup, fired up the car and pulled out from their watch point.

The Audi was keeping a moderate speed in the middle of the three lanes and Pender soon caught up, moved in behind and flashed his lights as an instruction to the driver to make his way leftward to the hard shoulder.

The Audi ripped right, into the fast lane, and Pender followed. The chase was on. The Audi was a faster car but his police Beamer, Pender believed, had the better driver. He kept a safe distance between the cars as they weaved in and out of the traffic and relished the coming chase when it became clear there were no conditions under which the Audi driver was going to let up. He knew suspects in car chases get away in over a third of cases, but they didn't from him, and this one would be no exception. He called his control room and was granted authorisation to continue the pursuit.

'OK, I've called in support cars and I'll get the chopper up if it's free,' said the call handler at the control centre. 'We should have eyes on him in about ten minutes, with a bit of luck. Don't lose him. The driver is understood to be a Peter Brady and he burnt his house down yesterday.'

'No danger,' said Pender as he shifted in and out of the traffic.

The Audi driver slammed on the breaks, careered across the motorway and exited the M1 at junction 10, still going at over 80 miles an hour. The car slithered from side to side and nearly went into a spin but was straightened and then slowed down before taking the roundabout onto the A1081 towards Luton, ignoring a red light and narrowly missing a taxi on its way to Luton airport.

Pender followed, called in the change of direction and fired up the siren now they were off the motorway – other drivers would need to be warned. He wasn't about to put anyone's life in danger, so had to take the roundabout at a slower speed. By the time he was on the A1081 the Audi was almost out of sight. He rammed his foot down on the accelerator – the chase was now on in earnest.

'Not going to lose this bastard,' he shouted to Olavarria as he increased his speed, until he saw a bright flash, moments before the sound of an explosion reached his ears. The Audi had not made the next roundabout. When the car hit the curb, it flipped and rolled several times before smashing into a tree and bursting into flames.

Pender called it in.

'You can call the chopper off,' he said. 'Brady's toast.'

The full array of emergency services were soon on the spot. The fire brigade, ambulance, police to seal off the area, more police to investigate the incident. DS Monika Dickens took control of the scene. By the time she'd had Pender's version of events, the flames had been doused and the car made safe, so she made an initial inspection of the wreckage. The dead body was charred beyond recognition. They'd have to go to dental records.

H heard the news on the grapevine later that day with a deep sigh and a heavy heart. He regretted more than ever his inability to bring the killer of Gill Brady to justice, and that there wasn't more he could have done for her husband. He went home, told his wife Julie about the case and went to bed after a scotch or two, full of the sorrows of the world. 'He deserved better. He was a good man. He didn't deserve to go that way,' he said to Julie, as he switched off the light and pulled up the covers.

***

The previous evening Peter Brady had made his way to Harlesden and pulled into the cramped car park of a small, seedy hotel, not famed for the refinement of its guests or the quality of its rooms. He made his way to reception and booked a room, paying with crisp notes peeled off ostentatiously from a big wad. He left the bag open on the counter in full view and, when he received his change, threw the money into it along with the keys to his shiny sports car.

He made his way to his room, threw his bag on the bed and left. He made it clear to the receptionist, in a loud voice, that he was going out and would be back in a few hours.

He never returned.

***

'You two take this one,' said Chief Inspector Hilary Stone as she walked out of her office and passed a note with an address to H. 'Happened fifteen minutes ago. One male gunned down outside a fried chicken outlet on Harlesden High Street. The uniform boys are on their way.'

'No name?'

'Not yet.'

'OK, on it, guv.'

H and his DS, Budgie McAllister, arrived at the murder scene half an hour later, dipped under the police tape, said hello to the uniformed officers and made their way to the body.

'Well, well, well, what comes around goes around,' he said to McAllister when he saw the corpse, 'and it couldn't have happened to a nicer fella.' He made an initial assessment: single shot, straight through the forehead. Death would have been near instantaneous.

'Well, Budge,' he said, 'if I didn't know Peter Brady died yesterday, I'd have put him in the frame for this. Mind you, horrible bastards like this Spiru normally have more than their fair share of enemies. Anyway, good riddance to bad rubbish.'

'Aye, boss,' said McAllister, 'the wheel of karmic justice has turned.'

H laughed out loud, and said, 'I swear, Budge, some of the things you come out with.'

H took out his phone and called Monica Dickens.

'Hello H,' she said, 'I was just going to call you.'

'Blimey, more karma – or what do you call it, Budge, when two people are thinking of each other at the same time?'

'Synchronicity.'

'Yeah, that's it. Well, I'm all ears, Monika.'

'Well, we finally managed to cut the body out of the car. I'm with the pathologist now. I was going to call to tell you because…well, the thing is, it's not Brady.'

'So you've checked dental already?'

'No, not yet.'

'How can you be so sure it's not him then?'

'Because it's a woman.'

***

He sat in the memorial garden; the gun he'd killed with placed next to him on the bench. He felt kind of OK. Not happy, nor even gratified, but better than he had since his wife had been taken from him. He was calm, and ready for whatever life threw at him next. He closed his eyes and took in the smell of the grass.

'Hi.'

'Hello Harry. I've been expecting you,' he said, opening his eyes.

Silence reigned for a few moments, until H said, 'I tell you what, Peter…I never had you down as someone who could do something like this.'

'I never had myself down as someone who could do something like this.'

'I have to take you in.'

'I know.'

'You'll be put away. A long stretch, to make it clear there's no room for vigilantes.'

'I know.'

'Good. OK. We're not going to have to mess about with handcuffs and all that palaver, are we?'

'course not – what d'you think I am, a criminal?'

H laughed and said, 'Good man. The thing is, just between me and you...'

'What?'

'I want you to know I understand what you've done. Under similar circumstances I'd have done the same. It wasn't your fault your life turned to shit…and if the system hadn't let you down…'

'No need to make excuses for me, Harry.'

'They're not excuses. You had a terrible break, and no one helped you.'

'You tried.'

'Yeah, but it wasn't enough, was it?

Brady said nothing.

H took out a pen and lifted the handgun from the trigger, opened one of the plastic evidence bags he always kept about him, and dropped it in.

'Come on then, mate. The car's in the side street over there.'

They walked slowly to the car. H opened the door of the front passenger seat and Brady got inside. H walked around to the driver's seat, got in and fired up the engine.

'So what's the score with the Audi?' he said as he pulled out onto the road. 'You give it away?'

'No, just made sure it got stolen, to buy myself some time?'

'And the gun?'

'They're easy enough to pick up these days, I find, if you've got a few quid.'

Some transformation, thought H. Brady sounded like a seasoned criminal.

'It won't be easy, inside. It's tougher than you might imagine.'

'Not as tough as it's been inside my head. I'm a free man, now, in here,' said Brady, pointing to his skull.

They were silent on the drive to the holding cell that would mark Brady's point of entry into the system, H reflecting on the idea that sometimes the only way a man can be set free was by taking the life of another. He'd been told often enough that revenge is a mug's game, that it makes things worse, opens old wounds, prevents people from moving on. Maybe in the long run Peter Brady would come to regret what he'd done, but when H turned to look at his captive he looked like a man who'd just drank deep from an oasis of sweet water after a long hard journey through the desert, and could now settle down to rest.

Funny old world, he thought, as he pulled into the car park of Harlesden police station in Craven Park.

'One other thing,' he said as they got out of the car. 'Why'd you only give him one shot? You told me you had visions of going to town on him.'

'Well, when Spiru's body hit the deck, it felt like the life went straight out of him,' said Brady. 'It felt over. That was all I needed…for his life to be over.'

THE END

# First Contact

# London: June 2013

Harry Hawkins, Danish pastry and Styrofoam teacup in hand, burst into the office twenty minutes late for the beginning of his shift. He took in the scene, and suddenly remembered what he'd been told before leaving work the previous afternoon, before his beer intake had gotten out of hand at the Rising Sun on Eltham High Street. Superintendent Hilary Stone spotted him immediately and noted the derision writ large across his ruddy face as she crossed the office floor, arm-in-arm with a glossy-looking young woman, to introduce him to his new charge. He'd never been one to hide what he was thinking, and it looked like he had no plans to start now.

'Ah, DI Hawkins, nice of you to join us. Meet DC Amisha Bhanushali.'

'Amisha, meet DI Harry Hawkins.'

'You forgot "the legendary" part, ma'am, if I may say so,' said H.

'Well, you're not looking all that legendary this morning H, if I'm honest,' said Stone. 'Though I have the distinct feeling a few hours with Amisha here may liven you up somewhat.'

Stone had told Amisha that Chief Inspector Hawkins had expressed reservations about her plans for the new partnership, and the newbie, who was already fully aware of both Harry Hawkins' legendary status and how little time he had for fast-tracked university graduates, held out her hand apprehensively. H shook it, in a perfunctory manner, sighed the sigh of the weary and took a hit on his tea. He nodded in the direction of a chair on the other side of the desk by which he was standing as he swallowed a mouthful of pastry.

'You can sit there. Welcome to the firm.'

He watched the new girl sashay around the table and set herself up in her chair, all the while replaying in his mind the talk he'd had with Stone the previous afternoon. 'Are you serious, Hilary?' he'd said. 'You're giving me some little slip of a girl? A student? To replace Little Danny with?'

'H, even Little Danny was a slip of a student once, was he not?'

'Well, that's as maybe. But…'

'No buts. This is a high calibre, extremely talented young woman. They don't come any better. She's serious, intelligent, hard-working, committed, and…'

'There's more?'

'Yep – she's got a PhD in Computer Science from Cambridge.'

H roared with laughter, and involuntarily spat tea all over the computer monitor he never used. 'Are you having a laugh? Is that what we're all about now? Computer science graduates? What's she going to do when she's out there, in that bloody jungle, with me? What's she going to do when some eighteen-stone growler comes at her with a baseball bat, fend him off with a floppy disc?

'I'm going to stop you there, DI Hawkins,' said Stone, showing him the palm of her hand. This is non-negotiable, and we don't need any of your ranting. Amisha Bhanushali is as resourceful as she is intelligent and educated. Calm yourself down. It is my considered opinion she has the skills and mindset that will complement your work, not disrupt it.'

'I don't need complementing, and anyway, she's an IT geek. Why does she want to get her hands dirty at the sharp end?'

'It's her ambition, the top brass have agreed the transfer and I've made my mind up. Discussion over. We'll try it for a month – and, by the way, no-one's used a floppy disc in twenty years. When was the last time you actually attended one of the IT training seminars we lay on for you?'

***

Gerry Adlington sat in his mini cab outside Croydon Town Hall. The car was a Ford Escort, basic version, no trimmings. He'd been frequenting the spot since he started out on his new career as a cab driver three months previously, having been forced out of a well-paid job in the local authority's housing department under something of a cloud. The company he worked for had an account with the council, which meant he always got paid, and the employees who used his services seldom, if ever, spoiled themselves one way or another on his backseat, or tried to rob him. He usually declined all other jobs when in the area, waiting until a council-employee fare popped up on his phone. It had been the toughest year of his life, the toughest by far, but he'd pulled himself together and was now getting back on top of things.

When the ping came he was on it in a flash, accepting the job and driving to the pick-up point.

'Fiona Richmond?' he shouted from his cab. The young lady nodded and squeezed into the back.

'Where to?'

'Purley, please, the council offices just past the train station.'

'Know it well,' said Adlington, 'what department you in?'

'What?'

'You work for the council, right? Just wondering. I've got a few friends in there.'

'Oh, erm, IT. I work for the IT department.'

'Oh, that lot. So it's you that sets up all those forms on the website nobody can understand?' said Adlington. The young lady in the back failed to register the humour.

'No, I work on the accounting systems. Purchasing, Council Tax, things like that.'

'Oh.'

Adlington's interest faded away, which was fine with his passenger – she was in no mood to enter into a conversation with the driver, preoccupied as she was with the urgent problem she was being sent to Purley to sort out. The rest of the journey passed in silence.

'Bye, then,' said Adlington as his customer, who was by no means a small woman, hauled herself out of the back of the cab.

'Bye.'

His phone pinged and he checked the potential new fare. A private address in Purley, no more than a minute from his present location. He declined the job, did a U-turn, headed back to central Croydon and parked up in his usual spot. There'd be other pickups from the offices soon. He was sure of it. So he waited.

***

'Where are we going?' said Amisha.

'Croydon,' said H. 'Another one's bitten the dust. I'm lead. The paperwork's on the chair, behind you. Read it.'

Amisha ignored it. ' Listen, guv,' she said, 'can I ask you something?'

'Fire away.'

'Is there a problem? I mean, do you have a problem? With me?'

'Nope.'

'Is it because I'm Indian, or because I'm a woman? Or because I went to university?'

'None of the above.'

'You do have a problem, then?'

'Listen, love. I've been ordered to play wet nurse so wet nurse it's going to be. I'll show you the ropes, teach you how to run an investigation. But just know that I do things in a certain way which means, from time to time, things can come on top.'

'Come on top?'

'Get ugly.'

'You mean violent?'

'Yeah, violent, and ugly, and…how can I put it – out of hand. From time to time. I'm talking about the sort of people and situations the classes at Hendon and the textbooks can't prepare you for.'

'And you think that when things "come on top" I won't be able to handle it or back you up?'

'I don't think it, DC Bhanushali,' growled H, 'I know it.'

***

The ping stirred Adlington from his slumbers. He fired up the Ford and was outside the council offices in less than a minute.

A young man of no more than twenty-five opened the door and scrambled into the back.

'Where to?'

'Coulsdon.'

'What end?'

'Library end.'

'OK.'

Adlington pulled out and headed for the town centre, planning to get on the Croydon flyover and then the A21 up to Coulsdon.

'What department you in. IT?'

'No, I'm with the child protection unit.'

'Oh,' said Adlington, swallowing hard and trying to control the sudden increase in his heart rate.

It was close to 3pm and traffic was heavy, so navigating the shoals of frustrated drivers was no simple feat. Adlington's sweat-soaked shirt clung to his back in the haze of the late afternoon. He reached the roundabout at the centre of town, doubts and second thoughts flooding his mind. He'd planned everything in detail. This was no time to lose his nerve. He exited the roundabout and headed for Shirley.

'You're going the wrong way,' said his passenger.

'Satnav's showing an accident just past the flyover, we'll have to go the long way around.'

Adlington watched as his passenger took out his own phone and fired up his mapping software.

'No mention of it here,' he said, looking up, 'are you sure?'

*Damn mobiles*, thought Adlington as he realised that he couldn't maintain the lie for much longer.

'I've got an advanced system here,' he said. 'I pay extra for it. It picks things up faster than the free ones on the phone.'

'Really?'

'Yep.'

'What's it called.'

'er…Easywaze.'

'Never heard of it.'

'Well, there you go – they say you learn something new every day.'

Adlington glimpsed at his rear-view again, and saw his passenger feverishly tapping away at his smartphone. His nervousness was morphing into anger at the kid's persistence.

'Why can't I find it? How do you spell it?'

'I don't bloody know,' said Adlington, forcing what he hoped looked like a jocular smile. He headed up Combe Road and turned left onto Shirley Hills Road.

'Where on earth are you going? This is the complete opposite direction.'

'Shut up.'

The kid's heart rate accelerated to match the driver's.

'Stop the car now. Let me out,' he shouted.

Adlington reached and grabbed the gun that had been stashed beneath his seat for weeks and pointed it at his passenger.

'Shut the fuck up, shut the fuck up or I'll blow your face off you right now.'

Adlington swerved into a narrow lane and dropped the gun as he fumbled to change gear, before accelerating up the single path to the top of Shirley Hills – a woodland oasis away from the noise and bustle of the city. He drove into a carpark and pulled up beside a black Kia Optima.

The kid in the back had seen the gun fall from the driver's hand but remained still, frozen by fear. He could taste the saliva thickening in his throat and feel the beads of sweat pour from his forehead. Adlington picked up the gun and jumped out of the car, a terrifying picture of half-controlled intensity, and clawed around in his pockets for the keys to the Kia and opened the boot before opening the rear door of the Escort.

'What's your name again, son?'

'Peter.'

'OK Peter. Out. Now. Get in the boot of that car.'

The kid wanted to run for the safety of the woods and the hills that now encircled them, but he didn't. He did the only other thing he could do, which was to pray.

'I said get in the boot!' Adlington barked.

'Why...what are you going to do?'

'Get in the boot, now, or I'll fucking shoot you. I'll do it. I swear I'll do it.'

For the first time in his life the kid understood the meaning of terror, real terror, as the boot slammed shut and plunged him into darkness. He heard the engine fire and felt the car begin to roll; he curled up into the foetal position and wished his brain would shut down, if only for a time.

***

'There you go son, get that down your neck.'

H handed a pint of London Pride to his old friend John Viney, who did as he was told as H sat down.

'How's your beer?'

'Not bad, H. Not bad. How's yours?'

'Handsome, mate,' said H, licking his lips, 'absolutely handsome.'

'Handsome is as handsome does,' said Viney with a smile. 'So... what you working on now – anything tasty?'

'Yeah, sort of. Some tosspot burglar breaks into a small two-bed terraced house in Thornton Heath. A kid, thirteen years old, wanders in while the tosspot's disconnecting the telly. The thief panics, smacks the kid across the head and does the off.'

John Viney sighed. 'Fatal blow was it, then?

'Yeah. Poor kid gets a bleed on the brain, dies in Mayday hospital two days later.'

'Jesus, mate, how do you deal with all this shit?'

'I just do, mate, I just do. Someone has to,' said H, finishing up his pint. 'Anyway, I don't suppose there's any danger you've got cash money in your pocket to get the next round with?

John Viney shrugged his shoulders. H knew the form. He forced his way to the bar and returned with two more pints.

'Anyway, I hope you catch the bastard soon,' said Viney, raising his glass.

'Well, it's not going to be easy with the new partner I just got lumbered with.'

'What, another one? What happened to that Danny geezer?'

'He's moved on to pastures new, mate. Canada. Now they want to team me up with a little whippersnapper of a girl. Another bloody Cambridge graduate they want to accelerate up the ranks.'

'Why?'

'Because she's Indian. And a woman. Why else?'

'But what's she like? Is she a sort, or what?'

'Well I wouldn't throw her out of bed to get to you, son – put it that way. And she's half-way to being some sort of genius, apparently, but she don't know her arse from her elbow when it comes to getting her hands dirty. This is what they're all like now – it's proper getting on my nerves mate, all of it. This one's spent most of her life behind a computer screen, far as I can tell. My guvnor's making me wet-nurse her for a month. At least.'

'It don't sound *so* bad.'

'Yeah, well, you don't have to deal with the scum of the earth like I do, do you? She ain't seen much action with me yet, as such, but when she does and things turn nasty, what's going to happen? I've been told to make sure she comes to no harm. How can I do my job properly if I've got to keep one eye out for these bloody soft kids all the time?'

'I'm sure you're up to it, mate. You said all this about Danny. And you didn't like that Scots bloke, Budgie, years ago. You ended up thinking the sun shone out of his arse.'

'Budgie McAllister was a Glasgow hard-nut, mate, underneath it all. He was the real deal – not some bloody spoilt, over-indulged middle class girl.'

'I suppose. Does sound like you've been lumbered with a bit of a snowflake this time.'

'Yep – and not a lot I can do about it. Anyway, get that down your neck, son. I've got time for one more. I promised Olivia I'd be home in time for dinner.'

***

Gerry Adlington pulled into his garage and jumped out of the Kia. He went through a makeshift door that connected to his house and made his way to the kitchen. He picked up the box of supplies he'd prepared, returned to the car and opened the boot.

'Who are you?' said the kid.

'Who I am is beside the point, Peter. Just get out of the car,' said Adlington, waving the gun around like he wanted to look tough but wasn't entirely sure how to use it. 'What's your second name, son?' he shouted.

'Braithwaite.'

'Well, Peter Braithwaite, do as I tell you or I'm going to kill you.'

'What have I done?'

'You, nothing.'

'So what am I doing here?'

'Never mind. Put these on.'

Adlington passed Braithwaite a set of steel handcuffs.

'Why…?'

'Because I told you to. Because I'm the one holding the fucking gun.'

Braithwaite complied and secured the handcuffs over his wrists.

'Get back in the car.'

'Not the boot again, please, I'm claustrophobic.'

'Back seat, just get in the back seat and lay down low.'

'Where are we?'

'You don't need to know.'

Braithwaite managed, despite the handcuffs, to twist his body into the back of the car. Adlington handed him a bottle of water and he slaked his thirst with it.

'Listen,' gasped Braithwaite when he finished drinking, 'I don't have a lot of money, but I can empty my bank account. I have a few thousand pounds I could…'

'I don't want your money.'

'What, then?'

Adlington said nothing. He loaded up the boot with something Braithwaite couldn't see, opened his garage door and returned to the driver's seat.

'You know Julie Travers?' said Adlington, checking Braithwaite in the rear-view.

'You mean The Head of Croydon Child Services?'

'Yeah, that's who I mean.'

'A bit. She's way above me. I don't move in her circles. We've been introduced though, I've said hello to her in the corridor. That's all.'

'Good enough,' said Adlington.

***

Adlington decided to drive from his home in West Wickham back through central Croydon on his way to the small cottage in East Sussex he'd hired. It was just gone 4pm and the traffic was building, but that didn't concern him. He dialled the number for child services.

'I'd like to talk to Julie Travers, please.'

'She's not available. Can I take a message?'

'No! I need to talk to her. Put me through.'

'Sorry sir, she's not available. If you leave your name and number, I can ask her to call you tomorrow.'

'Tell her to call me back, on this number. Tell her I've got her boy Peter Braithwaite.'

'Who?'

'I've got Peter Braithwaite, and I've got a gun. She calls me or he dies.'

'Sir…'

'Give her the message.'

Adlington shook with rage as he threw down the phone and picked up the gun. He turned and pointed it at his handcuffed passenger. For a second he considered using it and having the whole damn thing over and done with, but before he could call it one way or the other he felt the impact of his tyre on the central reservation as the right side of his car bounced into the air. The Kia would have suffered no more than a damaged wheel and axle if it hadn't veered to the wrong side of the road and collided, side-on, with a white van travelling in the opposite direction. Adlington's body was jerked forwards and smashed onto the dashboard as his forehead continued on it's inevitable meeting with the windscreen.

Two more cars tried to avoid the white van and failed. Both of them hit it at different angles in a four-way collision as the remainder of the traffic came to a halt on both sides of Park Lane, the main drag through central Croydon. The driver of the white van was the first to respond: a tall muscular man wearing jeans and a white T-shirt, and with a tattoo of a leaping lion on his right forearm, came out roaring his disapproval at the driver of the Kia. Adlington stumbled out of the car, produced the gun and fired two shots into the air.

Absolute pandemonium ensued as the crowd which was starting to gather around the accident dispersed in blind panic, heading in whatever direction would take them away from the bug-eyed, pistol-wielding lunatic.

This hadn't been part of the plan, Adlington reflected as people ran hell-for-leather away from him in all directions, but maybe the plan wasn't that important. This sudden turn of events had brought things into sharp focus and, if anything, steadied him.

He watched as Peter Braithwaite, a gash in his head seeping blood, struggled from the car, fell to the ground and got back to his feet. Braithwaite started to run but turned sharply when another shot rang out.

'Sorry, Peter. I'm still going to need you. Get back in the car.'

'No. *Please.*'

'I'm sorry. I really am, but I have to do this.'

***

H leaned across, keeping one hand on the wheel, and turned up the volume on the Dean Martin playlist they'd been listening to since leaving the Yard. This was their second ride together, but H had offered little in the way of active company. He preferred, it seemed, to fill the car with loud, cheesy music. So Amisha looked at her phone and, when it transpired that they were bound for Tulse Hill to 'see a man about a dog' before going on to work on the investigation, she decided it might not be best to ask whether the afternoon's activities amounted to the most effective use of the Murder Squad's time. But the way things were panning out irritated her, and being required to sit in the car like a child while H spent ten minutes in a nondescript-looking terraced house in Abbots Park did nothing to improve her mood.

H barely acknowledged her when he returned to the car, as he sparked up the engine and with it the Dean Martin playlist.

'Right, let's get down to Thornton Heath and see if we can't sniff this piece-of-shit burglar-cum murderer out.'

They drove on for a time, with H, despite the music, becoming more agitated with the thickening traffic on the outskirts of Croydon.

'This is all we fucking need.' Amisha looked on, unimpressed by his lack of patience and decorum.

By the time they approached central Croydon it had ground to a halt. 'I wonder what this is all about,' he said, scanning the scene – it looked like there was a police roadblock about a hundred yards ahead of them.

'Major incident,' said Amisha. 'It's early days – seems the whole thing blew up about twenty minutes ago – but, as far as I can tell it looks like a hostage situation.'

'Where,' said H, 'and how do you know this?'

'Up ahead, in the street. Shots fired by someone in a now-stationary car – a black Kia,' said Amisha. 'And I'm getting the information from our firm's online system – specifically, from looking at what the armed response units are up to.'

'You can do all that on your phone?'

'Yes, guv – all that and more. Our people have already moved from initial response to the consolidation phase. There's a cordon around the car.'

'Well…OK,' said H. 'Good work. We need to get closer and see what the boys on the ground are saying.'

H pulled up at the police cordon, jumped out and flashed his warrant card at the two uniforms on its perimeter.

'Alright boys, what's the situation?' he said.

'We don't have a lot of information, sir.'

'Well, has anyone been shot? Where the fuck is the gunman? Who's in charge here?'

Both of the PCs – who appeared to be even younger than Amisha Bhanushali – shrugged their shoulders and put on faces as blank as the day is long.

H turned on his heels, angry now, and went back to the car.

'Seems there's fuck-all we can do at the moment. We'll leave it to process,' he said as he fired up the engine. 'Most of the town centre's cordoned off. I'll get the siren going and we'll make our way round it.'

'I've got images,' said Amisha.

'What?'

'Whoever reported it, or maybe a bystander, has recorded the incident, or some of it, and they've put it up on Youtube.'

'What? Show me.'

Amisha held up her phone. H saw three cars and a van smashed up. In one of the cars he could just make out the two men, both sitting in the rear of a Kia. The images were grainy and indistinct, but the outline was clear enough. The camera started to scan the surrounding area. H saw a few characters milling about in the background, but the police on the ground seemed to have done a decent job in clearing the area. The image moved to the top of a building, where H saw shadows rushing across a rooftop. He strained his eyes to see if he could improve his view but before he could get anywhere the screen froze.

'What's happened?'

'Who knows?' These things come and go,' said Amisha. But she was immediately back into her phone, totally immersed in it, her eyes and hands flicking at speed and doing things H didn't understand. He sat and watched her in silence, perplexed but also becoming more interested in her, in what she might be capable of.

'I've found another one,' she said triumphantly after a minute of frenetic but concentrated activity.

'Another what?'

'Another video.'

This was from a different angle, and further away, and showed a team of police officers taking up a position behind two parked cars about four hundred feet from the Kia.

'That's Bob Crab,' he said, 'works for anti-terrorism.'

'I don't think this is a terrorist incident,' said Amisha.

'Why,' said H, who agreed with the assessment but wanted to hear the reasoning.

'Two guys in the back of a car, one's holding the other hostage. The kidnapper, he wants something. Something specific. My guess is this is not terror related. Looks to me like more of a personal thing.'

'Sounds plausible,' said H. 'Anyway, everything's in motion. I don't think there's anything we can do. Use your electro wizardry to find the best way around the roadblocks, will you?'

'Already done, guv. Left then third right should bring you out onto the ring road.'

'Okey dokey...nice work,' said H.

The clock was ticking. They were going to be late for the meeting with the police Informant H had lined up a meeting with. H made a call but got no response. He sent a text instead; Amisha watched him from the corner of her eye, as he jabbed at the tiny keyboard on his phone with his giant thumb and suppressed an urge to laugh. She went back to the examination of her own device.

'It's a hire car,' she said after a minute or two.

'What is?'

'The Kia. I grabbed the number plate from the video. It's owned by Croydon Car Hire and was hired last month, on a monthly rolling contact, to a Mr Marek Rybkowski.'

'How do you know that?'

'The car ownership is on the police database. I…'

'I know that, DS Bhanushali. I mean the Marek Rybkowski bit.'

'Oh, I just accessed the hire company's database.'

'How?'

'It's easy enough.'

'It's not legal.'

'I won't tell anyone if you don't.'

H smiled to himself but said nothing. This was an unexpected but welcome development.

'I assume whoever hired the car used a fake ID,' said Amisha, 'but I'll see if I can't track our Mr Rybkowski down anyway.'

'I know the firm,' said H. 'It's in Coulsdon, just past where we're going anyway. We'll push on to there first and have a little word with them.'

'OK guv, but shouldn't I just call in what I've found?'

'Yeah, call it in. But we're almost there, and things are probably moving fast, so we might as well lend a hand while we're here,' said H, forcing the car out of the traffic and into a side road, siren wailing.

A few minutes later they arrived at a drab site which was not much more than a car park with a prefabricated building on its outer edge that served as an office. A man approached the car as H was parking up.

'Sorry, sir,' he said. 'That's a no-parking spot. For the public, I mean. Can I ask you to…'

'Don't worry about all that, son,' said H, flashing his warrant card, 'We're not the public. I'm Detective Inspector Harry Hawkins. With the Met. There's a serious situation in progress in Croydon and I need car details. Black Kia Optima, licence plate number…DC Bhanushali?'

Amisha read out the number.

'Do you have a warrant for…'

'Listen, son. There's a man's life hanging in the balance as we speak. I need the details now.'

'I'll have to call the manager. He's off-site at the moment.'

'No, you don't. You have all the details we need in your files. If you make me come back with a warrant it'll be too late...and I will make an absolute fucking nuisance of myself, one way and another, and you'll wish to God you'd never met me. Am I making myself clear?'

The man said nothing.

'Right then, we'll catch up with you in the office in two minutes. Have the details ready for me.'

The man scampered away. Amisha looked across at H and almost said something. H sensed it and asked her if she had a problem.

'No, no problem, guv. I was just...'

'Wondering how I can be so unpleasant and heavy-handed with members of the public?

'Well, I wouldn't put it quite like that, but…'

'But,' said H. 'There's always a "but". Listen, I'll give you a "but" – but what if that was your mother tucked up in the back of that car with the man with the gun? Would you want me hanging round here all day being held up by some bloody jobsworth, or would you want me to get on top of the situation as fast as possible so we could get her the hell out of there? Which is it?'

Amisha said nothing but smiled and nodded her head a little. She'd been told by more than one person that Harry Hawkins was a dinosaur and a bully, and that he'd give her a hard time and deprive her of sleep. She could see what they were trying to say, but she was beginning to think that there might be more to him than met the eye.

H jumped out of the car, indicating with a wave of his hand that Amisha should do the same, and they went into the office, where they were presented with the paperwork requested.

'What the fuck is this?' said H to the man, now half-cowering behind the counter. 'Where's the ID? The passport number and/or ID card, or driving license? The entries are all blank on the form.'

'Er…I didn't do the work for this one.'

'Who did?'

'Er…'

'Make that call now. The owner. I need to speak to him.'

The man made the call and showed H with a nod of his head and facial expression that he wasn't getting any answer.

'No reply,' he said, after thirty seconds.

'Well, there's a fucking surprise,' said H.

'Guv, it's a fake address. It doesn't exist,' said Amisha, scrutinising the car hire agreement document and her phone.

'I want the phone number and address of your boss, now,' shouted H. The details were passed over and H checked them.

'He's only a few miles away, DS Bhanushali. Come on, let's get going.'

'It's not our case, guv. Shouldn't we just call it in?'

She was right, he knew, but H had the bit between his teeth now.

'No. We're on the scene. The outcome may well depend on speedy action. Let's go.'

H heard another car crunch along the gravel surface outside, and then another. He moved to the exit in time to see two police vehicles parking up. He waited for them to make their way towards the office, looking to see if he knew any of them. He did – they were led by DI Billy Jameson of the Met's counter-terrorism unit.

'H, what are you doing here?' he said.

'Well, we were out on a job nearby and we drove straight into it. DS Bhanushali here captured the number plate on an internet video and traced it to here. We were just passing, so thought we'd stop by. The Kia's been hired without proper details.'

'How did you find out where the car was registered so quickly?'

H pointed to his head and smiled. 'Ways and means,' he said, 'ways and means.'

DI Jameson knew he wouldn't get a straight answer and didn't have time to pursue the point. The two men exchanged a few more words until the new arrival was confident he knew everything H knew.

'OK H, thanks. Stand down. This isn't your case. We'll take it from here.'

***

'Gerry who?'

'Adlington. You don't even fucking know the name, do you? You took my boy, the last thing I had left in the world. You took my boy and you don't even know my fucking name.'

'Caller, I'm sorry, but I'll have to ask you to moderate your tone. If you insist on talking in this inappropriate way I'll have no option but to pass the details of this call, and the recording of it, on to the authorities.'

'What fucking authorities?'

'OK, that's it. I'm ending the call.'

'No, you're not. You've got my boy, I've got your boy.'

Julie Travers, against her better judgement, had returned the call on the off-chance it was serious. Now she knew it might be.

Adlington held the phone up to Peter Braithwaite's ear.

'Mrs Travers... Julie, it's me. Peter Braithwaite.'

'Peter?'

'Yes, the new guy, with the Family Support Programme. Please do what he says. He has a gun pointed at my head.'

Adlington moved the phone back to his left ear. 'Right. A straight swap. My boy for your boy.'

'Your boy? You mean you have a son who is with us?'

'I mean the son you took away from me.'

'You must know I can't do that.'

'Then say goodbye to your Peter Braithwaite. But turn on the TV first – you'll see I'm serious.'

'OK, Mr Addlington, I hear you. I'm going to look into this right now and get back to you. Please don't hurt Peter.'

'You have fifteen minutes. Call me back on this number or I blow your boy's face off.'

'They'll never bring your son out here,' said Braithwaite when Adlington ended the call.

'I know.'

'What, then?'

'The media will get hold of the story. Human interest. We'll draw a bigger crowd.'

'So you planned all this...all this chaos?'

'No. I was just going to hide you away in a little cottage in the middle of nowhere and negotiate for my son's return. Pretty stupid, when I think about it, but then I haven't been myself lately. But this has actually turned out better.'

'Why me?'

'I wanted someone from child services – that's all. Nothing personal.'

'What happened, why did they – we – take your boy?'

'I couldn't cope.'

'You must know they'd never exchange a boy in care for me.'

'Yeah. I've always known that, deep down.'

'What are you doing, then?'

'I'll have to end it.'

'You mean kill me?'

'No, Peter. I won't hurt you, unless you try to run or fuck with me.'

'So what's actually going on?'

'Wait and see,' said Adlington.

***

The order to stand down hadn't been easy to swallow. H thought he had something to offer but knew it wasn't his case so, reluctantly, he followed orders and once again set off for his appointment. Amisha, he noticed while he did so, was jabbing at her phone again.

'What you doing?' he said.

'Checking the emergency call database.'

'What, reading through 999 calls? That'll take ages.'

'No. I'm connected to the backend database, I'm running SQL searches for Croydon, gun, hostage…that kind of thing.'

'How did you get access?'

'I used to work in IT, guv, remember? I managed the latest upgrade to the system. I'm intimate with the database design.'

'Oh,' said H, 'don't they delete your passwords or something after you leave?'

'Well yes, they do, but…'

Amisha didn't feel nervous. She wasn't sure why. First week on the job and here she was breaking police protocol and telling her guvnor about it before she'd even finished. She realised what that meant – that she trusted him. She didn't know why, but she trusted him. The question was, did he trust her?

'OK, let's not beat about the bush. What have you found out?'

'There's still calls coming in, different perspectives on what's happening. And a gazillion more social media postings, but nothing that tells us anything new.'

'OK. Keep 'em peeled.'

She was unfamiliar with the phrase, but knew H's meaning well enough. Was he beginning to trust her? H continued driving at a steady pace until he reached a double lane road, pulled out onto the fast lane and put his foot down.

'Ten minutes and we'll be there,' he said. 'My grass – my informant – is getting restless. We'll need to settle him down,'

'I know what a *grass* is, guv. Anyway, this is interesting.'

'I'm all ears.'

'A call's just come in from a Julie Travers. Head of Croydon Council child services. Says the kidnap victim is her employee. Peter Braithwaite. She says the kidnapper called her. Something about wanting his son released from care and… Oh my God!'

H noticed her next reaction; it was impossible not to. It was as if a hypodermic of adrenaline had been emptied into her main artery and carried its load straight to her head, which was shaking in disbelief.

'The kidnapper. Gerry Adlington.'

H hit the brakes and spun the car, tyres squealing on the tarmac, as he skidded off in the opposite direction, firing up the siren with one hand and killing the Dean Martin tune with the other.

It was his case now.

***

Chief Superintendent Peter Meacher was hunkered down behind a police car a hundred yards from the Kia, deep in conversation with Mark Sliney, a police negotiator. Sliney had a loudspeaker in hand and was ready to go into action, although he had little to go on, when a sergeant made an appearance and said he had an urgent message.

'Sir, we're receiving information that the kidnapper is likely to be a certain Gerry Adlington.'

'What do we know about him?'

'So far, we believe he wants to negotiate a swap – the hostage for the return of his son, who was taken into care by child services. The hostage is Peter Braithwaite, a social worker for the council.'

'Why was the son taken into care?'

'Not yet certain, sir.'

'Anything else?'

'No, sir. The head of child services for the council is just getting someone to return to work to bring up the case files – she doesn't seem to know how to use the computer system herself and she's the only one left in the office. There's also a team at HQ researching Adlington's and Braithwaite's backgrounds as we speak, we should have more in a minute or two.'

Meacher, who was in charge of the operation on the ground, now turned to his tactical lead from the Specialist Firearms Command.

'Sergeant Williams, I need a tactical update. Where are we?'

'We have sight of both men in the car, sir. Both are in the back seat, close together. It looks pretty calm in there – we don't know which is which. We've had no sight of the gun.'

'Do we have a shot?'

'Yes sir, a clear shot from the east, facing the vehicle. We can take out either man without injuring the other, as soon as we have correct identification.'

'We need pictures, pronto,' said Meacher.

'We're on it, sir.'

***

H swerved past a BBC van and clipped a Sky one before screeching to a stop at the outer perimeter. The circus was in town. H pushed the car up close against the barrier and leaned out of the window to talk to its guardian.

'Alright constable, I'm DI Harry Hawkins, let me past. I'm up to speed on all this,' he said, flashing his warrant card.

'Sorry, sir, no can do. This is all locked down pretty tight. Orders are…'

H reversed the car a few yards, put his foot down, crashed through the barrier and onto the inner perimeter, where he was met by two armed officers. He and Amisha were barked at loudly and ordered out of the car by a voice H knew.

'Jack, let me past,' he said as he jumped out of the car, 'I know what's going on. I'm all over this, mate – you've got to let me through. I can sort it.'

'H, you know I can't. You're not part of this,' said Jack Thornton, 'Listen, there's more marksmen looking at you now than there are stalls in East Lane market – and for all they know you're a nutter in a suicide vest. That's what we've been hearing. We're all on a hair-trigger here mate, no one really knows what's going on. I suggest you get down onto the ground, slowly, before someone puts one through your nut.'

H could see the on-ground control group, approximately four hundred yards ahead. The kidnap site was a similar distance further on in the same direction.

'Let me through,' said H.

'No.'

'Then fucking shoot me,' he said, and broke into a zig-zag sprint.

***

The control team were massed around a computer screen, focused on a picture they'd just been sent by Julie Travers. They pulled up some high-resolution pictures they'd taken of the two men in the Kia. The negotiator had replaced the loudspeaker with a phone, now they had confirmed the number Adlington had used to call Travers.

'The shooter's the one on the left as we look at them. Confirm the positive ID to the snipers. Sliney, as soon as the snipers have had the message, call him.'

***

Gerry Adlington was all calm and poised as he watched the hordes of police and media people take up their positions. His phone had rung three times. He knew it would be the police calling to negotiate. It had been twenty minutes since he'd called Julie Travers and, he was certain, they would now know who he was. They would have a picture of him and cameras powerful enough to see into the car and confirm his identity. They could have taken him now, if they wanted to. It was time to up the ante.

His phone rang for a fourth time. He answered.

‘Hello, how can I help you,’ said Adlington.

‘Mr Adlington?’

‘Yep, that’s me.’

‘My name is Mark Sliney. I’m a negotiator. I’m calling to see how you are, and what you want.’

‘Nothing. I don’t want anything.’

‘How are you feeling?’

‘Don’t give me all that bullshit. I’m fine. I’m just about to kill Peter Braithwaite.’

Gerry looked Peter in the eye as he raised his gun. Meacher noticed the movement. Time to take the shot.

‘Don’t shoot, don’t shoot,’ screamed H as he came out of nowhere and rolled over the bonnet of a police car and into the centre of the control group.

‘Hawkins! What the bloody hell do you think you’re doing?’ shouted Meacher.

‘He won’t kill him. I know he won’t.’

‘What? How?’

‘It’s my case, his murdered son, it’s my case. I know him. He hasn’t got it in him. He’s just a broken man who’s lost one boy to a killer and one to the authorities. It’s suicide-by-cop.’

Meacher didn’t like Harry Hawkins, but he’d been in his company plenty, and trusted his judgement.

‘Sir, we have a shot. Repeat, we have a shot,’ said Smedly. ‘We can take him now.’

‘OK Hawkins,’ said Meacher. ‘You’re up. But if you get this wrong Hawkins, you’re finished. There’s plenty of people waiting for the chance to get rid of you – don’t give it to them.’

‘Yes, sir.’ H snatched the phone from the negotiator and stood up.

‘Gerry,’ said H. ‘It’s Harry Hawkins. Do you recognise my voice?’

'Uh…yeah. But I'm a bit busy now. I…?'

'I know how busy you are, mate. I'm here, in front of you by the police vehicles. I'm coming out.'

'Do not take the shot, repeat, do not take the shot,' shouted Meacher at the top of his voice.

H dropped the phone and walked into the open. The snipers kept their eye on the target. The cameras filmed the selfless hero. The story was getting juicier by the minute. H held his arms aloft as he walked to within shouting distance of the Kia. He felt the tension of the press and the snipers and the control group behind; but he wasn't tense himself, he was sure of his ground.

'Gerry, take it easy mate. I've come to help you get all this sorted out. The first thing we need to do is get the gun out of the picture.'

It wasn't destined to be a long negotiation with demands and counter-offers and delays, and H knew he wasn't in danger. If anybody was going to die in the middle of this it would be Adlington, either by sniper or his own hand.

H's job was to talk down a suicide.

'Why should I put the gun down?'

'Because you're a decent man, you don't want to see anyone hurt. Let Peter out of the car.'

'Why should I?'

'Because of your youngest – he'll need you.'

'They won't let me look after him, not after this.'

'Gerry, listen to me. You're struggling, I know that. You're hurting more than any man should have to. But if you get yourself killed here then your boy – Joe, isn't it – Joe's not going to have a dad for the rest of his life, is he? Is that what you want?' How old is he now?'

'Eight. But…I'm in no fit state to look after him anyway. That's why they took him away from me.'

'Maybe not at the moment, mate, but...these things can be sorted out. Things will never be the same, that's for sure, but your boy, your Joe, he can still lead a decent life…if you're there for him.'

There was a silence that seemed to go on forever as H let Gerry think things through.

'How will I get him back?'

'I don't know. We'll work on it. We'll work it out.'

'You don't have that sort of power…not after I've done what I've done today, it's all over for me.'

'You're right, I don't have the power. But I'll do everything I can. I promise. It's only over if you pull that trigger, or do something stupid. Then you die, here and now, and your boy grows up an orphan.'

Silence reigned again for a few moments, and then Adlington shouted, 'I'm letting Peter go.'

'OK. Good,' H replied.

H turned to the control group.

'He's letting Peter go. Don't shoot – this man will keep his word.'

Adlington fumbled around in his trousers, found the key to the handcuffs and undid them.

'Sorry, mate. Really sorry. Keep your hands up when you get out. One of them snipers might not be able to control himself.'

Peter got out of the car, kept his hands up and walked over to H, who nodded his head in the direction of the control group.

'Over there, son. You're doing great. Stay calm. Walk slowly. Everything's going to be OK.'

Peter nodded and did as instructed. He was alive. He was going to live. He reached the control group and collapsed in a heap.

'Good work Gerry, you've done a good thing there,' shouted H. 'Now, let's get you out of there…the first thing you need to do is throw the gun out of the car window, as far as you can. Then get out the car, backwards, feet first, and crawl backwards until we can all see you properly. Keep the palms of your hands flat on the ground at all times. Do exactly as I say – don't do anything, anything at all, to alarm the snipers. Have you got me?'

No reply came. The air hung heavy again with pregnant silence.

'Speak to me Gerry. Let me know you've heard what I said and that you're coming out.'

'OK, I'm coming.'

'Stop! Sling the gun out first. Right hand window. Then you come out the door on your left.'

Suddenly the gun came spinning out of the window, on the side H had indicated, and clattered onto the ground five yards out.

'That's great, Gerry, great. Now slowly out the other side. All hell will break loose, your job now is just to stay calm. Let everything happen.'

A few moments later the other rear door popped open and the soles of Adlington's shoes showed, followed slowly by the rest of him. As H predicted, all hell broke loose as armed policeman surged from every direction to surround him. He was forced to the ground, cuffed and dragged to his feet. H and Gerry caught each other's eye as Gerry was marched past.

'Keep your chin up, son,' said H. 'I'll do everything I can for you. I promise.'

H returned to the control group to back slaps and a round of applause. Even Meacher shook his hand and gave him a little punch on the shoulder, although he was more concerned about how to frame his report so he could get the lion's share of the credit for sending in the detective who had been working on the case of the kidnapper's murdered son. An unusual decision, but if he framed it right he'd pick up plenty of brownie points, and likely a commendation.

H was past caring about such things, and quietly left them all to it. He returned to the car, beckoned to Amisha to join him, and fired up the engine.

'I've never had a day like this before,' said Amisha. 'Not in my whole life. I've never seen anything like it.'

H remained silent.

'I mean, what you just did was…'

'It's not about me, Amisha. An innocent man comes away unscathed, a broken man lives to face his demons. About the best we could hope for, all things considered.'

'Permission to speak frankly, guv.'

'Always speak frankly around me, Amisha, and don't ask for permission again.'

'You'll be on the news tonight. Brave cop saves the day and all that. But you really don't care, do you?'

'I care about the people we're here to serve. And getting the people who hurt and exploit them out of the way. End of.'

'Yes, I get that.'

H was weary and in no mood for a heart-to-heart. He put the car into gear and set off for New Scotland Yard and the debrief.

'Come on, the sooner we get back to the office the sooner we can get out of it again and hunt down the bastard that killed Adlington's boy.'

***

'I've just been going through the timeline of the Peter Braithwaite kidnap incident,' said Hilary Stone in the office one morning three weeks later.

'And?' said H.

'And, I don't understand how you got to that hire company so quickly.'

H moaned.

'I already told you. It's in the report. We were in the area, news came over the wire. We went to help.'

'But you got there before the responding unit.'

'There was a lot of heavy traffic about, it must have slowed them down.'

'And the officers at the incident said you knew who was in the car when you arrived. If you factor in the distance you had to travel – and your Lewis Hamilton U-turn was captured on CCTV, so I know the exact timings – it appears you knew who was involved at the same time as the incident team. You must have had access to real-time information.'

'Well, call it a cross between copper's intuition and a bit of educated guesswork,' said H, with a shrug of the shoulders.

'Hmmm,' said Stone. 'I wonder…'

'Here you go, guv,' said Amisha, arriving at their desk and placing down a strong cup of tea with two sugars. She sat down next to him with her coffee. They'd been working the Adlington boy's murder case intensively since the kidnap incident. Amisha had watched H at close quarters as he coaxed, cajoled and occasionally threatened various denizens of the London underworld into talking about what they'd heard. This produced suspects who they then investigated in detail. Amisha had accessed a whole range of CCTV from shops and offices and found two of the suspects lurking close to the Adlington home on the day before the murder. H had that feeling he always got when he was closing in on a case. A bit more digging and they would be ready to make an arrest. He was sure of it.

'Anyway,' said Stone, 'enough of the kidnap incident. I came over to talk about Amisha's reassignment. The month's almost up and…'

'Woah, woah – hold your horses, ma'am!' said H. 'Let's not get ahead of ourselves here, we've still got a murder case to finish off. We're just on our way to an interview now, as it happens. Hurry up, Ames, knock your coffee back and we'll be on our way.'

'OK, guv,' said Amisha.

The two of them downed their drinks and H ran his hand across his mouth in appreciation.

'Nice cuppa. Let's get going, Ames.'

So its *Ames* now, thought Hilary as she watched them leave. Her instinct had been right. She allowed herself the luxury of a little smile as she made her way back to her office.

'What's so funny?' asked DI Graham Miller-Marchant when she passed his desk.

'Oh, nothing, it's just good to see the new girl managing to figure out a way of working with His Lordship.'

'Yes,' said Miller-Marchant. 'I've been noticing that as well. The odd couple. Beauty and the Beast. Who'da thunk it?'

'Me, Graham,' said Stone. 'I'd a thunk it. I *did* thunk it.'

THE END

# Amisha's Choice

# London: 2019

H crunched the numbers. A million crimes a year in London. That's an average of over 80,000 per month, 20,000 per week. That was around 3,000 per day. Boil it down further and that was around a few crimes every second. H was no statistician and had barely scraped through 'O' Level maths by the skin of his teeth, but he'd always maintained that was back in the day before schools gave prizes to everyone, when exams were difficult to pass.

Whether that was true or not, or whether his mental maths was accurate or not, didn't matter. He knew enough to know what the calculation told him, which was that statistically it was not unlikely for anyone to see a crime in progress. Especially if you were sharp and knew what to look for. Like H.

'Put them back,' he said to the man in front of him.

'What? Put what back?'

'You know what, silly bollocks…and tell your little mate over there watching the door not to step in and help you out. It'll only make things worse. For the pair of you. Trust me.'

'Who do you think you fucking are?'

'I don't think anything, son. I know who I am. Now – basically, I haven't got time for all this, so be a good boy and put it back.'

The man was thin and tall, a clear head higher than most people, with little black pissholes-in-the-snow eyes and sharp, rat-like features. The large Crombie overcoat he was swarming around in was at least two sizes too big, enhancing the comic effect of his presence. You couldn't have made him up.

Yet inside the coat, as well as the stolen goods, H sensed there was some muscle, a reasonable bit of strength. The shoplifter had the air of someone who knew how to look after himself in a squeeze. He returned H's stare with defiance for some seconds, before averting his gaze towards his boy on the door, and then the floor.

'You're Old Bill.'

'It doesn't matter who I am, son. Just put them back, like a good boy.'

"Like a good boy". The phrase irked, agitated, angered. The man looked to be about thirty-five years old and was not accustomed to being spoken to in such a manner. If this line of talk had come from someone with less presence than H it would have led to violence, but the man knew when to pick his fights, and when to back down.

He reached into the oversized garment and produced, with something of a flourish, two silk shirts. H was put in mind of old-school magicians pulling rabbits out of hats.

'Good lad – you know it makes sense,' said H. 'Now, fuck off, make yourself scarce.'

There it was again. Complete disrespect. Not the "fuck off", that was par for the course, but the "good lad". It was humiliating. He wanted to lash out, to teach this interfering old bastard a lesson. But he didn't. He again made eye contact with his boy and nodded towards the exit, signalling their retreat. Fight another day. The copper wasn't going to turn him in, so no harm done.

H was in a hurry. He made his way to the checkout, picked up and paid for his altered suit and barrelled out of the shop and into the multi-story car park. When he reached his level he saw, in the far corner of the great grey concrete space, the thin man with the ill-fitting coat, deep in conversation with his little pal. The air crackled with tension; something was about to happen. They seemed to be plotting, H observed. – maybe a little trip back to pick up the shirts now he was out of the way. On closer observation the discussion seemed to be about more intense matters. H could hear the pair of them, grunting like Orcs, although he couldn't make out the words. The thin man was angry, smarting from his unhappy, random meeting with a fat bastard of a copper out doing, as luck would have it, a bit of shopping himself. H watched on, until the body language made it clear: the thin man had been humiliated, and someone was going to have to pay for it.

H considered walking over to them, splitting them up, moving them on. But he didn't have the time. He made his way to his car, fired up the engine and headed for home.

When he arrived, he marched up the stairs immediately, to find Olivia dressed to kill in a long, flowing red dress. She was in the bathroom, applying the final touches to her make-up when H walked in.

As usual, thought H, she'd be the best-looking female guest at the wedding.

'Well, I've said it before and I'll say it again – you do scrub up a treat, love.'

Olivia took the compliment in good cheer – it was the best she was likely to get, and she smiled at her husband with deep affection.

'Never mind about me; did you get the suit sorted out?'

'Yep. Fits me like a glove now. The girl said I looked double-handsome. Said I put her in mind of Michael Buble.'

'More like Mr Bubble,' said Olivia with a laugh. 'You're so easy to butter up. Better put it on love and make sure it goes round your belly properly, we have to leave in ten minutes.'

'No danger. If you go down and make a quick cuppa, I'll be there in five.'

***

**Three months Later**

Veronica Gibson held her breath as she felt her daughter's hand squeeze tighter. This was the moment they'd both been waiting for – the verdict. The jury had deliberated for two days. What had they found to talk about? Surely the case was so clear-cut they could have made their minds up in ten minutes.

It seemed to take an age as the foremen stood, in ultra-slow motion, at the direction of the judge.

'Have you reached a verdict on which you are all agreed?'

'Yes, your honour.'

Veronica Gibson felt her daughter's fingernails dig deep into the palm of her hand and she responded by tightening her own squeeze. She was there for her cherished offspring, had been since the day of the vicious beating she took at a south-east London shopping centre three months earlier. The day that had changed both their lives. The wheels of justice turn slowly, but they *were* turning, Veronica reflected. The thought comforted her.

She looked at the defendant when the Not Guilty verdict came in. Stan McTavish. He was a thin, ugly and tall man, a good head above most people. He was smiling.

Veronica Gibson looked at her daughter and cried.

***

It had been a rough ride, far rougher than she could ever have imagined. Some days she felt she was getting better, and lately those days were occurring more often. But at other times she felt, deep down, that things might never be the same again.

She was just not sure how much was left of her old self. For months after nearly losing her life in the most horrible manner at the hands of Rufus Poundbury, her boyfriend-come-serial killer, her sense of self had been blown apart.

She'd felt like a distortion, a fuzzy hologram of what she had once been, unable to find her way back to solid foundations.

She considered the trajectory of her life: wonderful loving parents, outstanding at school, first class Honours degree from Cambridge University and her PhD in Computer Science from the same institution. She could have had a good life, a quiet life, working from behind her desk. She could have done well, just by using her powerful intelligence and guru-level IT knowledge to bring bad guys to justice. All from a harmless environment. She could have stayed safe.

But that was never the life she wanted. She'd wanted to put herself on the line, raise her head above the parapet – get onto the streets and mix with real people, be with them in the flesh, look them in the eye in their moments of desperation and anguish. So she pushed and cajoled and badgered the powers that be to move her from an intelligence desk job to the front line.

That's when she met him – Harry Hawkins. From that moment on her life had never been the same. She hadn't realised it at first, but hindsight was as clear as clear could be. Her strange, maddening desire to please him, to even be more like him, had led her to make judgements and decisions her old self wouldn't have dreamed of.

These days she thought back through the years. The highs and the lows. There had been highs, that she could not deny, but the lows had taken their toll. Breaking the law on multiple occasions because H had convinced her it was the right thing to do, deceiving all and sundry on his behalf. She'd done so much she could barely recall all the breaches of protocol as she tried to focus and understand each in turn.

Decisions have consequences, professionally and personally. The professional consequences were bad enough, but it was the personal cost that had brought her close to the endpoint, to where she was now. She had suffered more than most people could endure. She'd been kidnapped and raped by a member of a high-level paedophile gang, and lost Graham, her sweet, loving boyfriend, gunned down in a gallant attempt to help Harry Hawkins find his missing son. Those things hurt her so much, damaged her, made her so vulnerable that she was blind to the truth when she fell for the studied charms of Rufus, a killer who had used his not inconsiderable powers of persuasion on her for no other purpose than making her the final victim in his insane ambition to take the lives of eleven women.

These were the things that weighed heavily on her mind, the things she would never get over but had to come to terms with if she was to ever live in the world again – the things she'd spent months talking through with her friend and analyst Kasia Kotula.

She recalled their first session, the first step on her road to a tentative recovery, as she parked her car up a short distance from Kotula's treatment rooms near London Bridge.

'Hi Amisha, sit down.'

'Shouldn't I be lying on a couch?'

Kasia laughed as Amisha took her seat.

The therapy room was bare: two large leather chairs, a coffee table, soft lighting. No pictures adorned the light grey walls. There were no distractions.

'How are you feeling, in yourself?'

'What does that mean?'

'Day to day. How do you feel, generally?'

'There is no 'generally'. One moment I feel lost, another depressed. Sometimes I sit and cry. I get occasional moments when I feel a surge of optimism. But mostly I just feel empty and numb, like I barely exist. Have you seen *Sixth Sense.*'

'With Bruce Willis, yes.'

'That's how I feel, generally, empty and devoid of purpose, like one of those ghosts wandering around in limbo, unable to move on.'

Initially she'd thought the therapy would be a waste of time, that it couldn't help. She'd been around Harry Hawkins long enough for his ideas to have infiltrated her mind, most prominent amongst them the idea that you fixed your own problems, didn't go asking people for help when you had to face your demons, because it was a sign of weakness.

But the sessions continued, despite Amisha's low expectations. They talked and talked and she began to face the things that had happened to her. They worked through the pain and the grief and the sheer naked horror of being the target of a serial killer, of waking up on his sacrificial altar, bound and helpless. At some sessions she cried with lost innocence and at others she screamed and shook with rage and foamed with righteous fury.

The thing that worried her now, though, as she parked-up and headed for Kasia's new treatment rooms at Guys hospital, was whether her therapy had an end date; had she come to rely on it, would she need it as a crutch for life?

She walked through the doors of the bustling hospital, checked in at reception for directions and made her way to a small annexe at the rear of the hospital. The area was quieter and calmer than the main building, an oasis of peace at the heart of the metropolis.

'Amisha, hello. Come in.'

They started with the same question, more or less, that they'd started with those long months ago, the question about how she was feeling, generally, in herself. Her answer had changed.

'Generally,' said Amisha, 'I feel ashamed of myself. I feel humiliated. I've accepted what happened, I think, but I'm angry with myself because I was so naive and useless. I feel responsible, like it was my fault, like I should have known better. People say I'm clever, smart. Well, how smart was I, not to see that coming? All the signs were there...I just ignored them, blanked them out.'

Good progress had been made, thought Kasia. Acceptance meant she was moving forward through the process, though moving on from the shame and humiliation was still going to take time; especially with someone as proud of her abilities as this young woman.

Kasia directed the conversation to these feelings and they spoke about them for most of the session. They were nearing the end of their allotted time when Amisha broached another subject.

'...and there's another thing.'

'Go on.'

'I feel like I've let him down, that I'm not worthy of him.'

'Who.'

'H. I've been through more with that man than anybody in my life. Any relative or boyfriend. He knows things about me, and I know things about him. Secrets that are as deep as anything I've ever shared with a lover. Maybe more so.'

'Like what?'

There were things she couldn't tell Kasia, no matter how close they'd become. She and H, they'd eliminated bad people, when the chips were really down and when it needed to be done. She couldn't talk about the things that would compromise him.

'Things I don't want to talk about.'

'If we can't talk about it,' said Kasia, 'you'll have to find a way through it, on your own. Either that, or you have to sit down with H and tell him everything you feel about him. Good and bad.'

'I know, either that or...'

'Or what?'

‘Nothing. I’m off to lunch with him and Olivia now. I’ll start to figure things out.’

***

Stan McTavish looked as apprehensive as he felt as he walked into the main entrance of Guy's hospital and made his way to reception. He didn't like hospitals, even when just visiting, but hated them when he himself was the object of a doctor’s attention. His daughter, a sharp and well-educated girl who was wise beyond her fifteen years, had convinced him the insulin was the best course of action, the path that would keep him fit and healthy for as long as possible. Reluctantly, he'd agreed.

'Dad, you're not a well man. You don’t eat the right foods at the right time, and you never will. This way you don't have to worry, the system takes care of everything.'

'The system?'

Sally McTavish was reading on her phone about the most recent developments in pace-maker technology and drug-administration regimes. She’d been researching it, on his behalf, for several weeks and was determined to give him a nudge in the right direction.

'Yes. The system. You just have it fitted; it regulates your blood sugar levels. It's all automatic.'

'Automatic?'

'Yes, automatic. It takes away the guess work. All you have to do is go get it filled with insulin every once in a while, and then the computers and all that do the rest.'

'Computers? How can computers give me my medicine? I don’t know about all this, Sal.'

'Don't be silly, dad. This is the 21$^{st}$ century – what d’you want, some big old matron shambling around you with a stethoscope?'

'Well, now that you come to mention it…'

Conversations of this kind had persisted for months until Stan finally agreed to the operation, which had gone well. The technological marvel inserted into his body had been pumping insulin into his bloodstream for over a year, and although he'd never get over his fear of hospitals the operation had been a walk in the park in comparison to the horror he'd expected. Today was check-up day, insulin top-up day, as easy as checking, Sally assured him, the oil in his car.

The doctor, when McTavish was finally ushered into his presence, asked him how he'd been since his previous visit.

'Fine, doc…absolutely fine. Fit as a butcher's dog. Nae problems.'

The doctor performed the standard checks and concurred with the patient's overall assessment.

'Yep. All looks fine. You just need a little top-up. Go and see one of the nurses outside, they'll give you your refill.'

'Lovely,' said McTavish.

He was in high spirits as he left the treatment room and headed for the exit, until a sleek and luscious looking young Indian woman crossed his path and stopped him in his tracks. He was struck by her beautiful but aloof eyes; they looked straight through him and into the distance as she came towards him, looking about as tuned-out as anyone he could remember having seen. It was a heady mixture – of poise, beauty and utter disengagement with everything around her – and it triggered something in him that was not up for internal discussion or debate.

He let her pass him, turned and fell in behind her, and followed her out into the London sunshine. He made a mental note of her car registration number before returning to his own vehicle. No need to follow her now, he'd find her easily enough, when the time was right.

***

They were, of course, more than delighted to see her. H hugged her so hard he almost crushed the life out of her. Olivia broke down in tears. H got everyone sat down round the kitchen table, administered the wine and gave Amisha the update on the family and how Ronnie and Little Harry were doing. He was animated by almost boundless joy when telling the story of how the newly crowned British Welterweight Boxing champion, his cousin Terry Hawkins, came to lift the title. It was a long story, and Amisha knew the basics anyway, but it was a prodigious tale and no doubt H would be telling it prodigiously for the rest of his life. It seemed so incredible that a neutral listener would have to assume it was embellished beyond recognition but Amisha suspected, rightly, that much of the larger-than-life tale could nor would never be told, even to her. H was fastidious in protecting those who could come to harm – or the unwelcome attention of the authorities – if they knew about things they shouldn't.

As she listened, she saw that he had reached a place where once bitter things could now taste sweet, where the wind felt not cold but refreshing and the rain felt not depressing but cleansing. It was a place she understood, even if it now seemed far away from her.

Olivia, eventually, decided the story had gone on long enough and brought it to a close. The thing that interested her most was Amisha's wellbeing.

'So what's next, Ames? What do you plan to do once you've settled into the new flat?'

'I'm not making plans. Not at the moment. Just taking each day as it comes.'

'But you'll get back to the job, back to the Met, when you're ready?' said H.

'I don't know H. Really, I don't. I'm not sure I want to...or if they really want me, now.'

'Well, you just take your time Ames. Me and Olivia will always be here, anytime you need us. You're a long way from make-your-mind-up-time. Take it easy.'

'I know,' said Amisha, who decided that now was not a time to engage H in anything too deep and personal. She made her excuses and left after more hugs, kisses and professions of love and concern .

'Well, she's not perfect,' H said after closing the front door, 'but she seems a hell of a lot better than when I first went to see her at that funny farm.'

'H!' said Olivia, punching her husband on the shoulder, 'you know you can't say things like that anymore. Take that back.'

'Well...a funny farm is a funny farm – no point pretending otherwise. Anyway, she seems better, in some ways, but she's changed, hasn't she? More distant, colder. Like she's not really with us.'

'Well, what do you expect after what she's been through?'

'I know, babes. I know.'

***

Stan McTavish had few virtues, but he could be patient, and he liked to get things right in a situation if there was something in it for him. It was his third day of following the black-haired woman from the hospital. The London morning had broken, and the early mist was just being chased away by the rising sun when he saw her leave her flat. Amisha herself felt light and at ease; the week's session with Kasia Kotula had gone well, and the joy of seeing H and Olivia had been a real, long-lasting tonic. She felt as if she could almost smile.

She headed towards Clapham Common tube station, heading for a long morning walk by the river and lunch with her parents. McTavish followed her to the station but had no intention of following her into it. After she went in he gave it five minutes to ensure she was deep inside the labyrinth. He'd had a scare, once, when a target he'd followed to a station had returned to her flat to pick up her purse during his reconnaissance. But he learned from his mistakes, and after enough time had passed he returned to his car, took out a small bag of tools and made his way to Amisha's block.

Block entry was straightforward. He just hit all the buzzers and said there was a package delivery to anyone who answered until someone let him in, as seen in a hundred films and TV crime dramas. He made his way to Amisha's flat on the third floor, meeting an old woman who came out of her flat to greet him on the first, expecting a package. He assumed, correctly, that she was the one who let him in.

'Sorry, love. Buzzed the wrong bell, it's for the top floor.'

Gaining entry to Amisha's place was a piece of cake. This was the part he loved: the leisurely pouring over his target's personal artefacts, getting to know the sketches of their lives. But on this occasion, he felt disappointed. There were no pictures on the walls or anywhere else he could find – no personal possessions or mementos he could use to gain a glimpse into his target's life. The flat was clean and had the feel of a well-presented private doctor's surgery. This was the home, he saw, of someone who didn't want to be reminded of who they were, or maybe just someone who had never formed deep attachments.

He left the flat, spent a few minutes ensuring the Chubb lock was exactly as he'd found it and returned to his car, feeling as confident as the spider who has the fly securely trapped in its web.

***

Amisha gave her mother the deepest and longest hug that propriety would allow in a public space, kissed her cheek several times and then did the same to her father. Mr Bhanushali, raised in the old school, was not one for public shows of emotion, and had to fight hard to maintain his self-control and hold back the tears of love that seeing his daughter threatened to trigger.

They sat down at their table in a ridiculously over-priced, faux-Italian pizza place in Covent Garden. It wasn't the kind of place Amisha's father would have chosen in a million years, but it was what his only daughter wanted.

Amisha's parents – and Amisha herself – were not here to drag the past back to the present. They'd done that enough over the last months. They wanted, they needed, to move on; to talk about the future, to glimpse a shard of light, a ray of hope against the emotional carnage that Amisha had been through. They talked about her new flat and how she was settling down, until the waiter arrived. They all declined starters, selected their pizzas and decided to drink only water. It was a sobering occasion.

'So, darling, what do you think you will do now? You know you can always come back home, and work with us like you used to,' said her father.

'Yes, Amisha, that would be just lovely. Why not come home and stay with the ones who love you?' said her mother.

'Mum, we've been over this already. I need to move forward, not come back. I love you both so much, but it's not the right thing for me.'

'OK my darling. There's no rush. Let's just all take our time.'

The pizzas arrived and were devoured, and Amisha decided she wanted a desert.

'I'll have the tiramisu, please. Mum, dad?'

'Not for us, love. You have to watch the pounds when you get to our age,' said Mr Bhanushali, noticing his daughter looking at her phone below table-level as her sweet arrived.

'Always on the phone, Amisha. Some things never change…What are you looking at?'

'Oh, nothing much, mum,' said Amisha as she slammed her hand down with deadly speed and murderous accuracy upon a fly about to savour the delights of her tiramisu.

Her parents did their best to subdue their pangs of regret when the dinner was over and Amisha announced she had another meeting. They were hoping against hope that they could talk her into coming back to stay with them, if not for good then at least for a week or two while she adjusted to being back in the big city. Their daughter, as always the very model of an independent young English woman, had other ideas.

She sat back in the taxi taking her away from Covent Garden and smiled; lunch with her parents had done her the world of good. She felt in control, more ready to take on the world than she'd expected when she first left her place of convalescence just a week earlier. She tipped the cab driver generously when they reached their destination, jumped out of the car and headed to the entrance of Guy's Hospital. No need to stop by at the reception desk, she knew where she was going.

She looked up at the signs and saw what she was looking for:

*Diabetes and Endocrinology – Outpatients*

The sign indicated left at the next corridor.

***

The Eltham offices of *Hawkins and Hawkins, Private Investigators*, had not changed much since Amisha had last seen it – save perhaps for an additional eighth-of-an inch on the layer of dust that covered every surface. She found H alone, slumped at his desk over the South London Press and looking a little the worse for wear.

'So, H,' said Amisha, striding breezily across the room, 'here I am. Is Ronnie not about?'

'Nah, you're alright – I sent him out on a little errand after you phoned. What's happening? You alright?'

'I'm fine H – really. Making progress, I think.'

'Blinding! Glad to hear it. What can I do for you?'

'I just wanted to run something past you. I've been working on a little project and, as you like to say, it's my "make your mind up time". I have a decision to make.'

'I'm all ears.'

'Well…what's your take, on the trolley dilemma.'

'The what?'

'I did an extra-curricular course on moral philosophy when I was at Cambridge. It's one of the classic problems of ethical thinking. Would you kill one to save many?'

'Depends, on the circumstances,' said H.

'OK. You're on a trolley that's heading towards five people. It will kill them all. You have a chance to switch the trolley to another track, where it will kill only one person. What would you do?'

'I'd switch.'

'You didn't think about it long.'

'I didn't need to.'

'Most people give it more thought. Many decide that taking an action to kill someone is morally wrong, even if it involves saving others.'

'I don't think that.'

'You answered with the certainty of a man who has killed before.'

'Well…what d'you want me to say, Ames? You know my form.'

'Indeed I do, H – I might even call it *our* form. Now, say the one person was Olivia, or Little Harry. Then what?'

'I'd kill the five,' said H.

'You didn't dwell on that one long either,' said Amisha.

'I didn't need to. It's what I'd do. No question about it.'

'So the lives of the five are less important than the lives of your loved ones?'

'To me, yes. One-hundred percent. No danger.'

'Come here, I want to show you something.'

She opened her laptop and showed H a man sitting on a sofa, watching what looked like *The Great British Bake-off* on television and taking large gulps from a can of strong beer – what H would call a can of 'wife-beater'.

'Who's that? Am I supposed to recognise him?'

'Take a closer look.'

H narrowed his eyes and focused-in, and when the man finally let the hand holding the can drop from his lower face he exclaimed, 'I know him. Fucking hell, Ames, it's Stan McTavish. He got off scot-free from beating up a young girl. It was the same day I did…'

'Did what?'

'Did nothing.'

'I know. You gave evidence in court, but all you could do was pinpoint him as being at the shopping centre.'

'I never told you any of this. How do you know, Ames? What in the name of God are you up to?'

'He's been stalking me. He's hanging out in my flat when I'm out – making himself properly at home. I'd say he intends, at some point, to rape me, at the very least.'

'What…?' said H. 'What is this? Exactly what are you showing me here?'

'Is that all you have to say?'

'For crying out fucking loud, Ames, fill me in. I need more details. How do you know he's targeted you?'

'Because he's useless at it, and because I've become hyper-cautious. I spotted him the second he laid eyes on me and followed me out to my car at Guy's last week. Next time I saw him he was sitting in his car outside my flat. I have my own cameras positioned at strategic points around the block. He came and watched my flat several times. Then he came in, when I was out having lunch with my parents. He looked around, like he wanted to know more about me.'

'He could just be a burglar.'

'He didn't take anything, H, and he was at pains to ensure he left the place as he found it.'

'Why didn't you call the police?'

'I don't need them. And why would I? They'd arrest him for breaking and entering, and he'd be off on another hunt. No reprisals.'

'Reprisals?'

'Yes. I turned the tables, found out more about him. He has a chequered past. He's not just a shop lifter and a beater of women in shopping centres. Several reports of rape and indecent assault, but only ever one conviction. I'd even put him in the frame for some unsolved murders.'

'Do you have any evidence?'

'Nothing that would stand up in court. But how much do I need?'

'Ames…Where's all this going?'

'The thing is, he's targeted me. Do you understand what that means, H, after all I've been through? He's targeted *me*. I can't allow that to happen again. Ever.'

'Ames…what exactly is it you *want to run past me*? Can we get to the point?'

'Certainly. Well, as I already told you, it's my… make your mind up time.'

'Ames! I said get to the point…'

'He has a medical device, an implant, that controls his insulin levels. It's regulated remotely, by the hospital's online system. And getting into the NHS' 'encrypted' server, where the access codes are, would not challenge an ambitious fifteen-year-old.'

'What? You mean…?'

'You know what I mean H – don't be coy. I mean I could access it now, if I wanted to, through his wi-fi. Flood his system enough to kill him. Stone dead. We can watch him die, right here, right now. Nobody would ever know. Kill one to save the five, just like you said, Harry.'

H didn't like the tone of the "Harry".

'Just like you've done, when you've had to.'

'Ames, this is nothing like what I – we – have done in the past. You can't do this Ames, you know you can't.'

'Why?'

'Because you can't.'

'You've done it, before, on more than one occasion.'

'During moments of danger and emergency. This is just cold-blooded. He's not doing anything.'

'He targeted me, H. Given the chance, he'll hurt me, like he has others. Who knows what he might do in future, left to his own devices, when he's done with me?'

'Is that what this is about – revenge? On Rupert? Your moral, do-the-right-thing-trolley problem bollocks is just a smokescreen.'

H turned his attention again to the screen and saw McTavish haul himself up from the sofa, go into what looked like a bedroom and come out again with a packet of cigarettes, then into the kitchen and out again with a fresh beer before returning to couch-potato mode.

'The cameras follow him.'

'Yeah. Neat, isn't it? I've setup a full motion tracking system in every room. I have – as you are wont to say, H – got him by the bollocks. Of course, if I eliminate him, I'll have to go and uninstall it all tonight.'

'If you *what*…?' said H.

'If I eliminate him. Eliminate the threat – isn't that what we used to say?... I can eliminate him or…'

'Or what?'

'Or I hand everything over to our firm. They won't do much, obviously, and he'll go on to destroy more lives. So what do you think, H. What should I do?'

'You know what I think. You can't set yourself up as judge, jury and executioner and just go around killing people on a whim. Where would it end?'

'Wherever it needed to – whenever I decide. There is no end of evil scum out there, H, if I may quote your own formula back at you. And, as it turns out, I can kill people on a whim. I'm smart enough to go around killing pretty much anyone I want to.'

'But...'

'But what, H? You going to turn me in?'

'Of course not.'

'You're not going to turn me in because you don't care about justice, H. You care about retribution. That's all you've ever cared about.'

'That's not true.'

'I – we – could kill scores of proven, nailed-on paedophiles, murderers and terrorists all over the country, if we wanted to. Have you considered the possibilities here, Harry? All that evil scum, that you've hated and fought against so long…'

H stared at his protege. The sadness of the last months seemed to have evaporated from her eyes. She looked to be in complete control as her hands fluttered theatrically over the keyboard.

'One press of this key will do it, H…one little bit of pressure from this little pinkie of mine.'

H said nothing, just stared hard at the screen.

'So, H…guv,' said Amisha, smiling broadly. 'What do you say? Is it a go?'

'This is what I say, Ames,' said H, clasping his hands behind his head and leaning back into his chair. 'You can leave me right out of it. This is *your* fucking so-called trolley dilemma. You're a big girl now. It's "make your mind up time".

THE END

# Did You Enjoy this Book?

Thank you for reading our book. If you enjoyed it, won't you please consider leaving us a short review from the retailer you purchased it from. Reader reviews are extremely important for independent authors.

Thanks!

Garry and Roy Robson

# Get More Books

Thank you for reading our book. The whole *London Large* series has been great to research and write and we hope you enjoy reading it.

To say thank you we'd like to invite you to join our exclusive London Large readers club and offer you some of our work for FREE. All members of our club have access to free books and receive regular short stories before they are available elsewhere.

You'll also get news of all future releases at bargain prices before they become generally available. Joining is FREE, leave at any time.

To join go to our website at www.londonlarge.com - two ebook stories will be sent to you right away. You can read them on any device – PC, Kindle, smart phone, iPad etc etc

If you enjoy any of our books, please leave a review on the site you purchased it from. Reviews are about the most important way we have of finding new readers and it would be greatly appreciated. If you'd like to contact us, for any reason, we'd love to hear from you.

Write to us at Garryandroyrobson@gmail.com or visit and like our Facebook page here: https://www.facebook.com/LDNLarge/. You'll also find us at https://twitter.com/londonlarge

## THE LONDON LARGE SERIES

**Novels**

Blood on the Streets

Bound by Blood

Bloody Liberties

American Lockdown

Way Past Evil

Undefeated

**Short Story Collections**

Sharp and Short

Sharp and Short Volume II

**Boxsets**

London Large Series Books 1 to 3

London Large Series Books 4 to 6

## Non-Fiction

Making London Large

To find out more about us and our books or to read our blog on all things London and Crime visit our website at www.Londonlarge.com

## Harry 'H' Hawkins Timeline

| YEAR | EVENT |
|---|---|
| 1958 | Harry Hawkins is born in Bermondsey, south-east London |
| 1974 | The events of the short story *Tipping Point* |
| 1977 | The events of the short story *To Cardiff and Back* |
| 1978 | The events of the short story *On Tour* |
| 1979 | H joins the British Army – following the events of *On Tour* |
| 1982 | H fights for his country in The Falklands – as presented in the prologue of the novel *Blood on the Streets* |
| 1984/85 | The events of the short story *Counter Punch* |
| 1985 | H leaves the army |
| 1986 | He marries Julie, his long-time girlfriend, and joins the Metropolitan Police on a fast-track career path. |
| 1986 | The events of the short story *H Walks into a Bar* – set during H's first month in the police force |
| 1991 | H is made Detective Inspector |
| 1994 | The events of the short story *On Margate Beach* |
| 1995 | The events of the short story *That's Life*<br>H's first son, Ronnie, is born |
| 1999 | H's daughter Grace is born |

| | |
|---|---|
| 2000 | The events of the short story *Boy on a Bus* |
| 2001 | The events of the short story *Peter Brady* |
| 2003 | The events of the short story *Home Front* |
| 2005 | H is divorced |
| 2009 | H meets Olivia, who will become his second wife |
| 2013 | The events of the short story *First Contact* |
| 2015 | The events of the novel *Blood on the Streets* |
| 2015 | The events of the novel Bound *by Blood;* H is dismissed from the Metropolitan Police |
| 2016 | The events of the novel *Bloody Liberties* |
| 2017 | The events of the novel *American Lockdown* and the short story *Unsafe Space* |
| 2018 | The events of the novel *Way Past Evil* |
| 2019 | The events of the novel *Undefeated* and the short story *Amisha's Choice* |

# About the Authors

Roy and Garry Robson are, unsurprisingly, brothers from the Elephant and Castle, south east London.

Their father (variously a pig farmer, cab driver, haulage contractor and general ducker and diver) and mother (homemaker, cook and doctor's receptionist with a well timed left hook) raised them and their siblings with some old fashioned south London working class values. These included hard work, respect for their elders and a willingness to duck and dive when required.

One day, whilst enjoying a beer or two, they decided to write a Crime Thriller Series. They awoke the next day and were surprised to discover that they meant it.

Roy lives in Bromley and worked as a Service Delivery Manager for an International IT Consultancy. Garry lives in Krakow and is now, of all things, a sociology professor. Both career choices served as a source of confusion and humour to their parents, who were born and raised in the days before computers and sociology professors existed.

Harry 'H' Hawkins, the protagonist of the London Large novels, is not based upon Garry or Roy, neither of whom would survive the first chapter of a Harry Hawkins novel.

Website http://www.londonlarge.com
Twitter https://twitter.com/londonlarge
@londonlarge
Facebook https://www.facebook.com/LDNLarge
Email: mailto:info@londonlarge.com

Printed in Great Britain
by Amazon

58193293R00078